T0062168

SPANKED

SPANKED

RED-CHEEKED EROTICA

EDITED BY
RACHEL KRAMER BUSSEL

CLEIS
PRESS

Copyright © 2008 by Rachel Kramer Bussel.

All rights reserved. Except for brief passages quoted in newspaper, magazine, radio, or television reviews, no part of this book may be reproduced in any form or by any means, electronic or mechanical, including photocopying or recording, or by information storage or retrieval system, without permission in writing from the publisher.

Published in the United States by Cleis Press Inc.,
P.O. Box 14697, San Francisco, California 94114.

Printed in the United States.
Cover design: Scott Idleman
Cover photograph: **altrendo images**
Text design: Frank Wiedemann
Cleis logo art: Juana Alicia
First Edition.
10 9 8 7 6 5 4 3 2

Contents

INTRODUCTION: "A FANTASTIC KIND OF PAIN"

Just as I have a seemingly endless capacity to bare my ass and get it smacked soundly or make a squirming bottom hover on the edge of erotic oblivion with loud, ringing, stinging whack after whack, I don't think I'll ever get tired of reading stories about spanking. There was a time when I wasn't sure I could say that; after all, just how much is there to say about bending over and letting a firm hand connect with a pertly offered-up bottom? Or striking a pretty pair of buttcheeks so well the person beneath you moans in ecstatic agony? Well, as I've learned while editing this collection, there are an infinite number of ways to talk about the pleasures of getting spanked or spanking someone. While the actions may look alike, we all experience them differently and have different motives for indulging in this beloved kinky activity.

Me? I get off on just thinking about bending over for that special someone. Maybe I'm wearing panties, and only part of my bottom is visible. Maybe I'm not, and my spanker can see everything, including my wetness. I get wet at the mere idea of offering up my entire body to a lover to play with, tease, spank, and arouse. I've also had plenty of eager bottoms spread before me, offering asses that just begged to be spanked, whether they spoke words to that effect or not. But for me, and for many others, spanking is about much more than just the physical. It's about what that sensation creates inside of us. Spanking breaks down our barriers in ways even sex sometimes doesn't; it stirs up emotions; it makes us whimper or cry, or be proud of just how much we can take. It's primal and powerful, not to mention incredibly popular. I was thrilled to see spanking make an appearance on Showtime's "Californication," where the bratty, bossy bottom of a secretary demands that her boss spank her for any office infraction. "Hit Me Baby One More Time," indeed.

And those who bestow spankings, whether with hands, paddles, hairbrushes, or other devices, relish that power to bring pleasure and pain mixed together, to completely undo the person they are spanking with just a few (or possibly many) whacks.

The authors included here get just how intense spanking can be. Reading these stories took my breath away, and, even more so than my previous collections (*Naughty Spanking Stories from A to Z 1* and *2*), made me instantly horny. They've tapped into the beauty of spanking in a way that newbies, seasoned spankophiles, and those who are simply curious will be able to understand in an instant.

Rick Roberts opens this anthology with "Spanking You," a story I've read and reread numerous times, mesmerized by its rendering of a man so entranced by the vision he makes when he spanks his girlfriend, you imagine he could do it all night, every night, and never tire of it. He even offers up a little bit of a how-to for those would-be spankers looking for the courage to simply turn him or her over and begin this sensual process:

I used to tease you at the beginning of every spanking. As you'd kneel before me on the bed, not a stitch of clothing on your tan body, I'd fake the first blow—stopping just short of your ass, letting the air kiss your skin—and then place an affectionate caress onto your behind. By removing the certainty of whether the next sensation would be soft or a stinging slap, I'd keep you centered in the moment, keep you waiting and vulnerable, and your anticipation for the spanking grew. I would look down at you and smile, knowing that your desire for the first slap on your ass was growing unbearable by the moment.

Part of the thrill of spanking someone is being able to dangle what they most desire before them, to see them there waiting, panting, asking for it with body and soul, to know (or at least, fantasize) that they can't get off any other way than by the "punishment" you are about to deliver. Elizabeth Coldwell paints a portrait of a true top in "Through a Glass, Sharply," when she writes, "You have never really known power until the man you love is at your feet, naked or very nearly so, helpless and vulnerable, while you remain fully dressed and completely in control."

Madlyn March describes a first-time spanking in a way that will be familiar to any who have gasped, trembling, as they realized they not only can take, but crave, a whole lot more spanking than they'd initially expected:

I remembered how it felt when Mimi did it to me. At first, you're surprised someone's hitting you, even if you've asked her to. Then you're excited. Then you're in pain, but it's a fantastic kind of pain. Each slap makes you want more, as much as you can take, until you can't take any more, and you're shaking, more than ready to have an orgasm, the kind that can only be gotten from a woman diving headfirst into you with her wet tongue licking rapidly.

Any time an author can make me hot for something that in real life actually unnerves me, I'm sold. I'm not usually a fan of Daddy/girl stories, but in Teresa Noelle Roberts's excellent story, simply entitled "Daddy's Girl," she renders that role-playing relationship and its spanking potential perfectly, dissecting her characters' motivations while maintaining the magic they each hold so dear about their arrangement.

For some people, spanking is playful, almost silly—sexy in a way that makes you laugh as you come. This spirit is alive and well in L. Elise Bland's "The Breeding Barn," where a cheese paddle does double duty on the ass of an unsuspecting but happy boy bottom. And for the woman who goes by the name "Pink Cheeks" in the story of the same title, her fantasy comes true, to the letter, though in a setting she'd never have expected.

What I love most about this book is that while there are plenty of naughty boys and girls, that potentially clichéd setup never gets boring, because the authors take you right there, into the heart of a punishment spanking, letting you know that, on some level, each of these naughty boys or girls doesn't just deserve but needs to be spanked for his or her own reasons. The authors play around with these tropes, recreating the act of spanking until it morphs into something endlessly entertaining, just as a good top can keep a bottom on the edge, smacking harder and harder, then backing off, drawing out the play.

While I've subtitled this book, *Red-Cheeked Erotica,* what happens on the surface of the skin is just the beginning when it comes to spanking. There's an elegance, a poetry, a beauty to spanking that is much more akin to making love than fucking. It's a rhythm, a beat, a gracefulness, a way two people can connect without saying a word. These elements come together in M. David Hornbuckle's simple yet powerful "Still Life with Infidels #56," in which a planned kidnapping is set against the sparse backdrop of a steel mill as two recently reunited lovers attempt to recover what they'd lost.

The thrill of erotic spanking is nothing new, even if each time can make even the most experienced bottom feel like a blushing virgin all over again. James Joyce wrote a series of spanking-loving letters to his beloved wife Nora in December 1909 (and for a lesson in the art of sensual, utterly kinky yet romantic erotica, look up Joyce's naughty letters online). I cannot legally quote him here, but believe me, judging by these missives, Joyce was a full-on spankophile who understood precisely what it means to submit (and to willingly struggle).

As I already told you, when it comes to spanking, I simply can't get enough. I hope these stories turn you on, inspire you, and spark your own imagination about just how hot a spanking from someone who knows exactly what he's doing can make you.

Rachel Kramer Bussel
New York City

SPANKING YOU

Rick Roberts

The thing is, you can usually tell the first time you hang out with a woman whether or not she'll be into it. I'm not sure what it is exactly—maybe something in the way she responds to you, how she looks into your eyes when you're talking to her, how she hangs on your words and lets you set the pace in the conversation as if it's a dance and you're leading. There's something in her demeanor that silently conveys to you: *I'd let you do it to me...and what's more, I'd like it.*

I knew right away with you that first night, but I asked anyway. You were lying on your stomach, your shirt and pants and bra discarded beside us on the bed. I was massaging your back and legs, and as your cheeks lay exposed to me on either side of your black satin thong, I began to playfully pat your ass.

"Do you like being spanked?" I asked.

You laughed, but as I kept patting your ass, you shifted slightly to offer it more freely to me. A low hum, almost a groan, came from deep in your throat. It was the sound of someone who's just had an embarrassing secret discovered—feeling shame over the discovery but gratitude at having the burden of secrecy lifted.

Given this encouragement, I slapped your right cheek once, and then again, harder. The sound of my hand impacting your ass sparked the air. I heard you swallow your next breath. "It sends shivers up my body," you whispered. And just like that, we'd entered into a tacit agreement.

My hand and your ass. They made a perfect match.

I'd been told I have great hands for this. Maybe it was from years of playing tennis that I'd developed a deft touch for delivering spankings. The most effective stroke is not a clumsy, linear blow that jars the flesh, but one in which the hand practically stops before the skin and then ricochets upward at the end of the follow-through, much like a topspin stroke, leaving a stinging sensation spreading across the surface of the ass.

The best build for an ass to be spanked is not one that's firm and steel-tight, but one like yours—generously sized, with just a bit of cushion. With every spank delivered to a prominent ass, the force sends tiny ripples of shock up the hips and down along the thighs. When a woman is positioned on all fours, naked, with her hind region on display, she's at her most vulnerable. She knows you can see the most private places on her body, and she knows how it looks when she's being spanked. For you, this vulnerability was part of the thrill. Kneeling behind you, staring at the globes of your ass stretched out in front of me, I knew you *wanted* me to spank you. I knew you wanted me to make your flesh quiver under the force of my hand, and you knew that I knew this. And you would deliver your ass to me again and again, both of us intoxicated in this knowing of knowing.

I used to tease you at the beginning of every spanking. As you'd kneel before me on the bed, not a stitch of clothing on your tan body, I'd fake the first blow—stopping just short of your ass, letting the air kiss your skin—and then place an affectionate caress onto your behind. By removing the certainty of whether the next sensation would be soft or a stinging slap, I'd keep you centered in the moment, keep you waiting and vulnerable, and your anticipation for the spanking grew. I would look down at you and smile, knowing that your desire for the first slap on your ass was growing unbearable by the moment.

With you, the act of submitting yourself for a spanking was especially profound. You had body issues: you thought your ass was too big ("my big fat ass," you used to call it in dismay) and your hips too wide, and your thighs showed hints of cellulite. Bending over and presenting your naked hind regions summoned all kinds of insecurities. But I also knew this added an extra dimension to the act. In getting spanked by me, you received affirmation. Every stroke from my hand delivered a message of acceptance: *my* hand chooses *your* ass.

Propped on all fours, you knew *everything* was on display. The tiny opening of your anus stared at me indecently; so, too, the lips of your vagina. I'd often have you spread your legs wider apart so that I could get a better view. My spankings never failed to bring you to a state of arousal, and I would watch with fascination as your labia became wet and engorged to the point of an almost animalistic excitement. This was the curious paradox about spanking sex: that the vagina is almost an afterthought. When you became too aroused to ignore, I'd slip a finger between these lower lips and then take it out and trace a line across your ass or thigh, marking your skin with your own fluids.

Sometimes I'd take it one step further. As you knelt in front of me, presenting yourself to me, I'd grab you just below the ass and spread you even further apart. And you would sigh gratefully, loving the sensation of being so completely on display, open and unguarded, an exegesis of ecstasy.

It was the series of two or three strokes placed quickly together on the same area of skin that brought you closest to the edge. I'd slowly work up to them, spanking you at a deliberate pace, switching from cheek to cheek, dispersing attention to the entire surface of your ass. Then, as you were primed for more and a rosy-pink hue had spread across your cheeks, I'd start in— usually on the right one. *One-two. One-two-three.* Bunched together, just like that.

It was the intensity that got you, the white-hot feeling of one on top of another on top of another. I'd deliver these slaps and then wait a second as they reverberated throughout your body and left you in an audible shudder.

It was all about the ass, but one night, my hand strayed down to your upper thigh. "I'm spanking your leg now," I said, stating the obvious to gauge your reaction.

"Yes, you are," you said in a haze. From then on, spanking your thighs became a regular part of our sessions.

Not long after that, we began experimenting with body spankings. You were proud of your breasts—barely C-cups, perfectly proportionate to the rest of you—and when you fucked me on top I loved watching them bounce up and down so unrestrainedly. One day, I started slapping them—playfully and lightly at first, and then not so lightly. You orgasmed more quickly than ever.

Then, finally, the last taboo: we were lying in bed with my

hand between your legs, stroking your pussy. I lifted my hand before each stroke, slyly petting you there. Your legs fell open. I started spanking your vagina softly.

"Look at this—I'm spanking you between the legs," I said, as if narrating an out-of-body experience.

"I know," you said naughtily.

I began to spank your pussy with the same force as if I was spanking your ass. You closed your eyes and your mouth fell open. I kept at it until you couldn't stand it anymore. You moved your hand downward and found your clit and grabbed your breast with your other hand, enjoying your body as it lay consumed by heat.

Your last spanking came a year after we broke up. You'd ended up at my place again one night, and soon we found ourselves falling back into bed together.

"Get on all fours, sweetie," I told you, as I had told you countless times before.

You hesitated, your body issues flooding back to you, but you did as I said. "Do you like what you see?" you asked, seeking assurance. You were sensitive about the swell of your stomach that hung down just above your thong, but to me it just added to your vulnerable beauty.

"I do," I said. I started to spank you and heard your familiar shivers and sighs.

I pulled off your thong and exposed the naked crevice of your ass once again. You received my spankings in ones and twos and threes, shaking with pleasure.

That was the last time you and I were together. By that point, our relationship had reached a point where we couldn't go back to the way things had been before and we couldn't go forward. But I like to think that the bond that we'd formed still exists. I like to imagine that in some ecstatic dimension, you're forever there: propped in front of me, naked and unguarded, ready for me to set your ass and your soul on fire.

PERFECT BOUND

Shanna Germain

It's the librarian look that gets them. They walk into my little erotic bookstore expecting—what? I don't know. Not me. Not this tall woman behind the checkout counter in her twin set, glasses hanging by their silver chain, swinging into that laced space between her breasts each time she moves. They're not expecting this dark up-do of hair, these swept-to-the side bangs that half-hide my dark eyes. The long black skirt, slit so that it seems to promise a glimpse of thigh, of more, if only they could see behind the counter. They're not expecting this cliché, this proverbial boy's wet dream. Not expecting me.

I can tell by the way they move their eyes toward me, and then away, like I'm just another book on the shelf. I've seen boys look at porn with the same denial of fervor.

Take this boy. Not a boy, really. Twenty-five if he's a day. Tight black jeans over his skinny legs and ass. Torn gray T-shirt that says GETTING LUCKY IN NEBRASKA. A small silver piercing rests just under his thin, pale lips. He'd be emo—I keep up on these things, make it my job to know—if not for the naturally blond hair.

He's been here before, but only to browse. Today, it's different. He's looking for something. I wonder which of his friends clued him in. He circles around the checkout counter for a while, picking up books and looking at them without looking at them. Opening them wherever the pages fall. Cracking spines. Smudging ink with his thumb.

I keep doing the thing that I'm doing. It looks like paper-work, but really it's just little squiggles on paper, something that lets me keep my eyes busy. Something that lets me lick the end of the pencil, tongue the lead just a little.

He makes smaller circles, like a cub playing at predator. Instinctual. Clumsy. Big feet and his smell on the wind.

I look up from my squiggles and tuck my pencil into my up-do.

"Can I help you find something?" I have my dark red lipstick on. The color that says *Open me. Take a peek inside.*

"Oh, just looking," he says. Looking as he says it. Brave boy. Big blue eyes.

I lick my teeth, show the flash of white against the dark. I reach into my hair for my pencil, pull out one long, loose curl that falls down against my neck.

"Well, if you don't need anything…"

"Wait."

"Yes?"

He lowers his eyes and picks up a book from the counter in front of me. It's *The Art of Spanking*, by Milo Manara. The boy's palm covers the illustration on the front cover. He flips the book sideways and runs his finger down the spine.

Now comes the break point. Will he ask, or will he leave here with only a book to tide him—and me—over?

The boy swallows. I can hear the sound as loud as if it was

my own throat. He slides the book across the counter toward me. His fingers tap-tap the book's cover.

"I hear you specialize in...binding," he says. "Printing."

The word he's looking for is imprinting, but I let it slide. "I do. Do you have something you need...bound?" I give him back the pause he's given me. The emphasis.

"Please," he says. Something so soft in his voice, so painful in his need. Even his body sags with the letting go, the asking. His shoulders soften.

I reach across the counter, touch one of his fingers as it covers the book. "Something in particular?"

He bites his bottom lip, making an indent in the pink curves. There is a space of time, two or three seconds, where he can still back out. Buy the book instead. I wait.

"Me," he says, finally. "Me."

I smile at him with my dark lips and my white teeth. I pull the pencil from my hair, and the barrette with it, and a layer of dark curls falls down around my face.

"Flip the sign then," I say. "I charge by the hour."

He shakes his head, and his hair shifts across his brow. "I don't..."

"You can come in and sort books." I think of how many boys I already have sorting books. And dusting. I have a pretty dark-haired boy who does my books—in the money sense—and one who does my taxes. "Or something." I point at the door with my pencil. "Flip the sign."

While the boy—I'll have to ask his name at some point—flips the sign in the door from OPEN to SHUT, I open the drawer in front of me. It's filled with rows of old typewriter ribbon. I have a man who buys them for me wherever he can find them—auction houses, garage sales, estates. He sends them to me by the boxload. I pay him for his costs and shipping, and I bind him and bend him over my knee whenever he comes into town.

I like the ones on spools, with nylon ribbons. Black. No lift-off tape or colored ink. And they have to be truly old. Not just replicas. A bit of ink gets on my fingers as I find the one I want.

The boy is back. I shake loose the rest of my curls with ink-smudged fingers. His eyes follow the movement. I take the type-writer ribbon in one hand and the book he's chosen in the other.

"C'mon back," I say.

The chair in the back room is the one I like best. It's antique, I think, with an ornate back and a red velvet cushion as a seat cover. Taller than most chairs today and no arms—that's the important part.

I sit. When I cross my legs, the fabric of the skirt slides open. His eyes follow that movement too.

"Have you done this before?" I ask.

"N-no. No."

"You understand what happens here? You understand that once we start, we don't stop?"

"Yes." Surer this time.

I unspool the end of the typewriter ribbon so that it falls to the floor like curls.

"What's your name?"

"Stephen, with a *p-h*."

"Well, Stephen with a *p-h*, how did you get here?"

"I live just around the—"

I sigh. Boys. Sometimes they're the perfect thing in the world. Other times...

"No, who told you about me?"

He sticks his thumbs in his belt loops. "My friend Anthony."

Of course. Anthony. He's one of my window washers. Pretty, pretty boy with cocoa skin and a piercing fetish. Comes by once a week or so. I have a brief, delightful image of getting the two of them together, under my thumb, so to speak. I'm getting ahead of myself though. We'll have to see how this session goes first.

"Get undressed."

This is the moment when some boys hesitate. Some ask questions. Some go home. Stephen with a *p-h* just starts to undo his belt. All of his nervous energy is transformed into the process of taking off his clothes. He does it carefully, the belt through its buckle and the slide out of his jeans. I'm not a sub, but if I was, that movement, that sound, would be enough to get me wet. I wonder if he knows this, if he's played that way before or if it's just something that comes naturally to some people.

I unspool the black ribbon all the way while he undresses. By the time I'm done, the ribbon covers the floor around me and he's standing before me with his lean white body. Only his chest and cock have any color in them, rosy red, both.

"Come closer." I shift my legs again, let the skirt's slit slide higher.

I'm tempted to start at his cock—it juts out at me, asking to be touched—but I'm afraid it will send him over the edge too soon. Instead, I wind the ribbon around his thin waist, replacing his studded belt with this thin black line. Around and around his waist, just below his belly button, down toward the brown hairs that rise up his belly, down toward the place where his torso meets his thighs. I work around his cock, never touching it, pretending it isn't there between us.

When his waist is wrapped, I snip a short piece of ribbon off and reach to his wrists. I put them in front of his body, loop them together, and tie it off.

He is so obedient that I wonder if he's paying attention, if he really understands what's happening. His eyes are closed, and the tip of his tongue plays softly at the corner of his lips. I run the sharp edge of my nail up between his thighs, and he takes a sharp, quick inhale. Fully here then. That's good.

I cup his balls in my palm. They feel full and solid, like living Ben Wa balls. I roll them softly, watching his cock pop each time the pad of my thumb hits the underside. He's a sigher, sending out soft exhales of air, so quiet that they're hardly audible. I wonder what he'll sound like when I really get started. Will he stay quiet? Or can I break the noise from him?

I make the first loop of ribbon around his balls, and he opens his eyes. The wet pink of his tongue finds the corner of his lips again. I wrap him all the way up, from the soft curves of his balls to the wide base and finally all the way to the small flared tip. There's so much ribbon that I have to double-wrap in places.

When I let go, he looks down at himself. No words. Just the way his cock jumps again, the way the head is shiny and slick. I know it won't be long before he starts leaking onto the ribbon, before he wets it enough that it will mark his body with its ink. I wear black skirts for a reason.

"Lie down." I'd pat my lap, but he's already moving. He puts his bound hands over his head, without me having to tell him, and then he lays himself across my legs.

He weighs less than I expected and I didn't expect much. His cock presses into my thighs. And he's got a great ass, full and curved, despite his lean build. The black ribbon around his waist accentuates the white globes of his buttcheeks. I run my palm across the pale skin, finger the space between his cheeks. I can't hear his sighs, but I can feel them, in the push of his ribs and belly against my legs.

I draw back my hand and lower it on the fleshy part. Not hard. Just testing. A little smack, a little pink against that pale. Again. Still no sound. No movement from him. His cock doesn't change against my lap. Either he's in over his head, or he's ready for more. Sometimes it's hard to tell the difference.

I cup the curve of his ass in my palm again. I love that place, the curve of skin and muscle. Those little dimples that only boys seem to have. His body relaxes against mine. Sighs into relief. That's my cue to start again, my hand coming down hard and fast, so fast that my palm stings. He wiggles, pressing his cock harder into my thigh, trying to escape the blows, trying to move closer to them. Above his head, his bound hands close on the air.

When I stop, his breathing—not sighs now, but something heavier, louder—fills the room. I press my finger to one of the pink marks on his skin. He clenches his ass and lets out his first words.

"Holy fucking shit." His voice is filled with both awe and discomfort.

"Oh, Stephen with a *p-h*." I have to laugh a little. "We've only just begun."

I put one hand on the back of his neck, bend him just a little so that his ass rises higher, his cock presses harder. I start at the rounded bottom of his ass, covering the pink marks that are already there. His skin is warming up, or my palm is. With each stroke, he shudders just a little. He tries to give his feet a hold on the floor, but I have him bent so that he can't quite reach.

The skirt material is thin enough that I can feel the edges of the typewriter ribbon that I've wrapped around him. I know it's chafing him now, rubbing against his skin in a way that is both pleasure and pain. I open my legs a little beneath him, creating a hollow for his cock between my legs. He rubs into the space, tries to settle himself into a rhythm.

I spank the backs of his legs, the inner area of his cheeks, slow and steady. The sound of my palm against his flesh, the way he wiggles under my blows—is it so bad to say how much I love it? How much I live for moments like these, boys like these? If I were to slide one finger beneath my skirt right now, I know how wet I'd be, how open. But that's for later. I don't want to fuck this boy, I just want to do this, raise my hand to him again and again. I want to imagine him later, when I'm alone, his pinkened skin and his ribbon-wrapped cock. His quiet, submissive desire. I want to see him sorting books later in his skinny black jeans and remember this moment, him squirming and sighing across me.

The book he chose earlier is next to the chair, and I lean over and pick it up. Hardcover. An art book, so it's heavy and wide. Not as much noise and sting as a softcover, but a lot of heavy pain. I crack it against the side of his ass first. He inhales sharply, and raises his head to try and look at me.

I push his head back down and grab the ribbon at his waist to hold him steady. Already, the ink has marked his flesh, imprinted his struggles on his skin. They're beautiful, long black strips of ink filled with potential for words and stories. Desire made visible.

The book makes a flat sound against his skin. Nothing like the sharp slap of my palm, but strong in its own way. His sighs get louder, turn to low moans, and then, finally, to soft words. Gods and oohs and fucks that slide out of his mouth as though he can't help himself. I don't think he can.

Finally that word that I wait for, the soft whisper. Please. I pretend I don't hear it—the book is loud against his flesh, getting louder, getting faster. His back is all muscle and tension as he tries to get comfortable, tries to guess where the book might land next. Please, he says it again, even as he's trying to get loose. His cock makes my skirt wet, his string of please, please, please, makes the rest of me wetter.

I drop the book. I need to get closer to this again, back to the sound of my hand on his ass. Back to marking his skin with the sting of a slap. I'm faster with my hand, more precise.

This time, when his feet dig for a hold, I let him have it.

For a second, he's off balance, surprised to find himself with any leverage at all. And then he's fucking my lap, rubbing cock and ribbon against me. He rises up to meet my hand, lowers himself to meet my lap. He does all the work now, and I let him, focusing on placement and speed.

His *please*s turn to *fuck-fuck-fuck*s, and I know he's going to come. I wish I could see his cock, wrapped and rubbed a little raw, as he lets go, but it's enough that I can imagine it. It's enough that I can see his ass clench tight under my hand. I tighten my grip on the ribbon, use it to help his momentum. I up my spanks, faster and harder, meeting his ass each time it rises, and then giving a sharp hit on his downstroke.

Soon, he comes the way boys do—loud and quick, and drenching the front of my skirt. The room smells instantly like sex and sweat and come. While his body shivers and pumps, I softly stroke the sore places on his skin. Small bruises—from the book, likely—are beginning to show through the pink. He's going to feel this every time he sits down for the next week, maybe longer.

He lies across my lap for a long time while I stroke his skin back into the memory of softness. After a while, my thighs start to ache. The rest of me is already aching for my fingers, the memory of him behind my closed eyes. Later, I tell myself. Wait. Keep this pleasure.

"Stephen, it's time to get up," I say.

"Oh, oh, yeah." When he slides off of me, his grin is all boyish, but not flustered or embarrassed. Not anymore. Chest and cock still jut, still pink, with more power now, not less.

I brush a hand over the front of my skirt where the fabric is wet. My fingers come away ink-stained.

"Here, let me cut that off you." Careful with the scissors, I cut through the ribbon at his wrists and waist first, and then slice against the softening skin of his cock. He doesn't flinch, not even when the scissors touch his skin. "There you go."

I gather up the ribbon that has fallen from his body. I'll use this later, remembering. I admire my handiwork across his body— black ink, pink handprints. I wonder what he'll think of later, after, when he undresses and sees the marks I've left on him.

"What about you?" he asks.

"Tuesday afternoons," I say. "You can wash windows." Him and Anthony. I think they'll work well together.

"No, I mean, what about *you*." He actually points in the general direction of my skirt, which makes me want to laugh. Someone is training these boys well long before they come to me.

"You're off the hook for now," I say. "Next time."

He actually looks a little sad. "Oh, okay."

I pick up his book. "I'll wrap this up for you to take home. Come on out when you're ready."

By the time he comes out, I've tucked my hair back up in its up-do. I've reapplied my lipstick. I have my pencil between my lips, the taste of lead in my mouth. My glasses are tucked between my breasts. He's looking, not-looking at me again.

I slide the book across the counter to him. "I hope you enjoy this," I say. "It's been bound quite beautifully."

His face actually goes pink, from the cheeks on up. The reminder of the color sends a small shiver through me.

"Oh, and flip the sign on your way out, will you?" I watch him walk out, remember that ass beneath my hand. When the door shuts, I lean over and start making squiggles on my paper. I'm expecting the dark-haired boy who does my books any minute now.

BETTY CROCKER GONE BAD

Alison Tyler

When Simon came home for lunch one day and found me cooking naked, he didn't know what to do. We'd been living together for three months, but for some reason, he'd never been home when I'd baked. Which shouldn't have been a big deal at all, except for this fact: I always bake in the nude. It relaxes me.

"What's up, Dana?" He eyed my apron, the rounded tops of my breasts barely hidden, the curve of my waist accentuated by the tightly tied apron strings. I had flour on my arms and chocolate on my lips and my fingers were sticky with dough. The oven had made the kitchen hot, and my cheeks were flushed and pink, easily seen because I'd tied my long, black hair off my face with a rag ripped from cheesecloth.

"Baking cookies," I told Simon innocently, turning to get a stick of butter from the refrigerator and letting him see that I had absolutely nothing on aside from my KISS THE CHEF apron. The ties hung down my naked back, tickling my ass when I moved.

He stepped closer. "Are you almost done?"

I shook my head and moved around him to the baking tin. Greasing the pan slowly with the butter, I said, "Once I put these in, I've got twelve minutes before the next batch can follow. I have about three batches worth of batter…so I'll be done in about thirty-six minutes."

I said the words flippantly. I knew what I was doing.

He watched me scoop spoonfuls of chocolate chip cookie batter onto the sheet. Then he waited for me to slide the tray into the oven. I looked over at him, wondering what he was thinking. I didn't have to wait long.

Simon picked up one of our clean rubber-coated spatulas and motioned for me to walk to his side. "Bend over," he said, his voice taking on that low, husky moan he gets when he's horny. "Bend over and touch your toes."

"Now?" I asked.

He nodded.

"We've only got twelve minutes," I reminded him.

"Set the timer."

Swallowing hard, I set the timer on our stove and then hurried to his side. He crossed his arms and waited, and slowly I bent over and offered him my bare ass.

"Pretty thing," he said, staring at me, moving the string of the apron aside to further admire my nakedness. "How often do you cook in the nude?"

"Just when I'm baking," I whispered, bending over as far as I could, feeling my hair tickling my toes. "I only like to bake naked."

"So every time we've had cookies…"

"Yes, and cakes, and zucchini bread—"

He ran one hand over my ass, then gave me a light slap. "That seems sort of naughty to me."

I could see the tips of his black boots, and then they disappeared from view as he walked away. I didn't know what he wanted me to do, so I stayed where I was. Then I heard him drag the kitchen stool over to my side. In a flash, he'd hauled me over his sturdy lap.

"I'm going to give you a paddling for being such a naughty girl," my boyfriend said. "We'll keep it up until your timer rings."

I couldn't help but turn my head. The clock let me know that I had nine minutes and thirty-four seconds to go—one heck of a paddling. I took a deep breath and waited for the first stroke. He brought the rubbery spatula down hard on the left cheek of my ass, then again on the right.

Even coated with rubber, the implement had no give. Every stroke sounded loudly against my ass, and in moments, I was moaning. I knew better than to cover my ass or to beg Simon to go easy on me. So I did my best to stay still, gasping great cookie-scented breaths as the chocolate melted in the oven.

After a few more strokes, Simon had me bend over and grab my ankles, and he went to work even more ferociously, punishing the backs of my thighs, the rounded curves of my ass, making me groan as he hissed, "Such a naughty girl. How else have you played when you cook?"

I thought of the time with the blender. I had innocently filled the machine with the makings of a milkshake, and then leaned my panty-clad pussy against the vibrating body of our old-fashioned glass blender. I'd started with the first setting, the simple, always useful WHIP. (The word alone can get me in the mood.) That was nice. It had the effect of the lowest setting of my vibrator. I upped it one, to PUREE, and then one more, quickly, to CRUMB. This was better—humming along as my milkshake whirled around. I especially liked the coolness (from the ice cream) mixed with the vibrating motor.

When I needed an extra push to bring myself higher, I upped the speed to CHOP, then GRATE, then BLEND. (Most vibrators I've owned have had two or three speeds. My blender has seven.)

After climaxing at LIQUEFY—followed by a little heavy breathing, and a quick adjustment of my skirt and nylons—I'd opened the blender and poured out my milkshake (something no vibrator can offer).

"Tell me, baby," Simon demanded.

I described using our rolling pin, impaling myself on our cool, marble roller, thrusting over and over until the tool had been completely drenched with my own personal blend of honey.

I told him about finding a pair of towel clamps that hadn't been attached to the wall yet. The clamps were coated with a smooth and sleek metallic paint, and I immediately placed one on each of my nipples. They pinched deliciously.

Between stinging strokes of the rubbery spatula, I told Simon about playing with our corn-silk husker (which is the softest of all kitchen brushing utensils). This little brush is more delicate than many made-for-the-job French ticklers. After I'd come against the blender, the husker felt sinfully light on my still-humming clitoris.

Simon seemed slightly shocked, but I could tell from the gravelly sound of his voice that he was even more turned on. So I told him secrets.

The wire whisk had been next on my list of masturbatory devices. I'd heard something, somewhere, about the handle being inserted into a woman's pussy and then the bulb being tapped to create a sort of "twangy" interior effect. I had tried it and found that the tuning fork effect was quite unexpectedly pleasurable. I'd had visions of Simon putting one in my cunt and one in my ass and playing me like some sort of perverted musical instrument.

When I told him that one, Simon laughed, liking the image. He took a step back and I turned my head, catching a bit of him reflected in the window of our oven. He was admiring his work, and he quickly turned me so that I could have a view of my hot, crimson bottom.

"Check the cookies," he said, his voice low, as if it were the most erotic command ever given. I took a deep breath, stood, and opened the oven. The treats were almost done, but not quite. While we waited for the cookies to finish, Simon began riffling through our drawers, stacking item after item on the countertop.

"It's been too long since your last punishment, hasn't it, Dana?"

I nodded.

"We'll take care of that today," he assured me. "Two more twelve-minute sessions, coming right at you, baby."

I stood back, pressing my hot ass against the refrigerator, watching as he pulled a box of plastic wrap from the drawer and placed it next to a new pair of rubber gloves, a wooden cutting board with a handle, a pair of scissors, and a roll of cheesecloth.

"Put the new batch in," he said. I hurried to obey, carefully lifting the cookies onto a rack to cool, adding spoonful after spoonful of chocolate chip dough onto the next sheet.

"Now, come here."

I walked to Simon's side and he instantly had me over his lap again. This time, however, it was the cutting board that landed against my naked bottom. And, oh, talk about pain! He smacked me repeatedly with the thin, hardwood paddle, turning my ass a deeper, more perfectly-toned hue of cherry.

Checking the timer, he said, "On your feet, Dana." I stood and he removed the cheesecloth from my hair, tying it instead as a gag between my lips. He kissed away a bit of the chocolate from my mouth and then hoisted me onto our Corian kitchen counter on my stomach. With a gentle grin, he folded one of our dishtowels and slipped it under my hips for padding. He took a pair of oven mitts and slid them under my cheek. Simon loves to spank me, but he takes care of me, as well. I was as comfortable as any sub can be waiting for a punishment session.

"I'll get the next batch," Simon assured me, pulling the roll of plastic wrap from the box and cutting off a long sheet. This he wrapped around my throbbing buttocks, having me lift up off the counter to assist him. Tightly bound, I felt my cheeks pulsate, and my pussy begin to fill. I couldn't remember being this excited before.

The bell rang.

"Hold that thought," Simon said, expertly lifting each cookie from the tray and scooping out the last batch. He flipped on the timer again and turned to deal with me, pulling something from our kitchen junk drawer that I couldn't see. Then, softly, he said, "Grit your teeth, Dana, this is going to hurt."

I did what he said. Simon never lies to me.

The sting of the unknown implement startled me. I'd been expecting the paddled feeling of the cutting board, or the smarting smack of the wooden spoon. Instead, it felt as if he'd used a crop on me. I tried to turn my head, but he placed one hand on the back of my neck and pushed me down. Next, the sting came on the backs of my thighs, a few smarting strokes in a row. I squirmed on the counter, writhing, begging through the cloth gag to know what it was he was using.

"What is it? Simon, please." Somehow, I thought that seeing it would comfort me.

"A wooden chopstick," he said, dropping the item and picking up a new one, a thicker one. This I immediately sensed was the handle of a spoon, but I didn't have long to contemplate it. The weapon hurt in the same way a cane would, a quick pain followed by a lasting throb each time it landed on my wrapped asscheeks. I howled through the cheesecloth gag.

While I was moaning, Simon reached for the rubber gloves and slipped one on. I've always been an aficionado of rubber and vinyl. Being punished with a rubber-gloved hand had me screaming, my cries echoing in our kitchen. The pain was wicked, and the sound of the rubber meeting my plastic-wrapped skin almost made me come.

But I wanted something more. I wanted to feel those rubber gloves against my naked skin.

"Please," I begged Simon, pulling the cheesecloth gag from my lips so I could speak. "Cut it off me. Let me feel it."

He quickly cut through the plastic wrap with our kitchen scissors, freeing my ass for a new kind of spanking. My cheeks were already throbbing, but I still managed to raise my hips off the counter to meet each blow. The rubber felt indecent against me, even more so when Simon let his rubber-covered thumb slip between my asscheeks to brush my pussy.

"Oh, god," I moaned.

"You like that?" His thumb made a quick rotation around my clit, and then he pushed inside of me. My pussy clenched on his rubbery digit, and I groaned as he slipped out his thumb and slid three fingers into me instead. My eyes were wide open at this brand-new sensation. Rubbery fingers fucking me, thrusting into my dripping wet pussy.

But Simon wasn't ready to reward me just yet. Once he brought me right to the brink of climax, he resumed the spanking, now using a rubber-gloved hand that was wet from my own juices. Simon gave me quite a few smacks before the bell rang for the last time. He ignored it, rolling me over instead, pressing his lips to my pussy lips, which were still covered by the plastic, licking against the plastic wrap coating my cunt.

I sighed and arched my hips up, not able to decide which felt better: the cool Corian under my butt or Simon's warm lips on my delta of Venus. Then he unwrapped me, peeling the plastic away from my warm, wet skin. No more debating; his lips felt magical around my pulsing clit.

"The cookies..." I whispered, but Simon was deaf to this chef's pleas. He kept working me, playing me, until I came....

At least we had two batches that didn't burn.

LASER TAG

Madeline Glass

The first time he spanked me, I thought he was a pervert. The second time he did it, I wondered if I was. By the third time, I was certain that both were true.

We met at a concert. He was with his friends in the row behind Tricia and me. They were acting completely juvenile—using little laser pointers to draw ridiculous spastic spirals on the backs of people standing further down in the theater. It was a loud rock concert, one of my favorite bands, and while everyone there was yelling and whistling and clapping, I found the antics behind us so annoying.

I turned to face the group of four men and yelled, "Dudes, cut that out, it's really distracting." I'd caught the tall one with his laser held in front of his body. I looked down and saw a tiny red dot on my jeans. While I'd been turned with my back to him, he'd been drawing stupid circles on my ass. "How objectifying," I thought to myself, and then smiled. I had worn my new jeans and I had to say, my butt looked great in them. Still, this was childish and ridiculous. I looked up and glared at him. He quickly retracted the laser and stuck it behind his back with a sheepish grin. He had twinkly eyes and straight teeth. I don't know why I notice those things first, but I always do.

Satisfied that my stare-down had had the desired effect, I turned back to the show. "Stupid boys," I muttered to Tricia.

Two minutes later, the shirt of the guy in front of me was alive with swirls again. I tried to ignore it. The whirling dervishes of little circles got more and more insane, and finally I spun around and snatched the laser from the tall one's hand, saying, "Give me that!"

He looked surprised, and then satisfied, knowing that he'd pressed the right button. I had fallen right into it: the way he looked at me made me feel not superior, as I had planned, but borderline vulnerable and sexy, and in trouble, all at the same time. I put the light in my pocket. Soon after, the group of boys was gone.

We ran into the tall one after the show, standing outside the theater. He saw us and started walking toward us, calling out, "Hey, you stole my laser! Give it back!"

I laughed at him, noticing his build and eyes and teeth again. "You just don't give up, do you? It's mine now. I took it away for your own good."

His eyes softened. "Listen, I'm sorry my friends and I pissed you off. Let me buy you a drink to make it up to you. I promise to behave. I'm Nick." He stuck out his hand. I took it before I even realized I was doing it, let the surprisingly warm, surprisingly elegant hand envelop my own, and introduced myself. "Colette. And you can buy me a drink, and one for my friend, and if you behave, I'll give your little toy back."

"Fair enough. Nice to meet you, Colette."

We walked to the bar around the corner. I shot a glance at

Tricia, that "don't you dare leave me with this dude" look that girls use with each other.

Nick was, as it turned out, not only endowed with mischievous eyes and perfect teeth, but also, in the absence of his friends, well mannered and nice. As we talked, I was becoming smitten, imagining what it would be like to feel his hands on my face, his lips over mine. How does that happen, anyway? I tried to stay cool, to keep the conversation light and bouncy, but every time he looked at me I felt naked and exposed, like he knew exactly what I was thinking.

When Tricia got up to go to the ladies' room after a couple of rounds, I excused myself and followed her. She'd had enough and wanted to leave. I really didn't want to go, and I was comfortable staying by myself. "If you're sure," she said. "I really need to get to bed; I've got work in the morning."

I assured her that I'd be fine. "Go home to bed," I said. "I'll call you in the morning."

"You call me tonight if you need to."

I returned to the table alone.

Nick and I had another drink, and my heart flipped when our fingers brushed past each other on the table or our feet inadvertently touched. Eventually, the inevitable happened: Nick said, "You want to get out of here? I live a couple blocks away." I demurred, saying I wasn't sure that was a good idea. He replied, "If it makes you feel better, I live right next to the police station, and I promise to behave."

Well, how could I (and three strong cocktails) argue with that?

He paid the tab and we walked past my building, past the yoga studio on the corner and a block over to his place. He turned the key to the brownstone and led me upstairs. The place was immaculate, with quality furniture and Buddhist art. Not

what I'd typically expect from a frat boy type who behaves
badly at concerts.

We sat on the black leather couch and his hand went to my
thigh. "These jeans are going to get you into trouble, you know,"
he whispered.

"Oh?" I feigned ignorance. "And why is that?"

"Because you look so killer in them. These legs, that ass...
and," he continued, "this front pocket here," he traced the
outline of the laser, "has something that I want."

"I think you've behaved yourself well enough to get it back,"
I said. He reached into my pocket as I leaned back into the cush-
ions and pulled it out, using its tip to trace a line from between
my legs up to my lips. I kissed him then, and he pulled my body
over his on the couch so that I was straddling his thighs. His
hands went to my hips and brought them down to his lap. His
cock was hard through his jeans.

"You know," he said, between kisses, "you shouldn't take
other people's things without asking. It's wrong." I giggled
nervously. "It's not funny," he continued, his cock getting harder
by the second. "It's very wrong to steal."

His hand pulled back and smacked my ass, landing firmly and
holding its place there for a few seconds. I yelped and laughed,
"Hey, that's not funny! That hurt!" He did it again, this time
harder, and moaned softly when his palm hit and I flinched
and gasped. *What the hell?* I thought. *Who is this guy?* But the
warmth that his hand had produced on my skin felt strangely
good, and my pussy squeezed itself involuntarily, throbbing
against the tight denim, wanting more.

His cock was straining against his jeans, and I pulled back
to look at him. His face was serious; his eyes had lost all
mischief. "Do it again," I whispered. He smacked the other side
of my ass, and I moaned with the increasing intensity, feeling

my pussy getting wet, both of my asscheeks radiating heat.

He growled, "You're a naughty girl for stealing, aren't you?"

The slaps had stopped, and I realized that if I wanted more, I'd have to play along. "Yes, I am, I'm a naughty girl for stealing."

"And you need to be punished, don't you?"

"Mmm, I need you to punish me. I was wrong to steal from you. It was such a bad thing to do." I wanted this to happen—I wanted to feel vulnerable and sexy and in trouble with this man who had so expertly turned the tables on me from earlier in the night.

"Stand up and take off your jeans."

I backed off the couch and stood in front of him, slowly unbuttoning and unzipping and sliding the stiff fabric down my legs. My ass burned, and I let the jeans fall to the floor, stepping out of them and running my hands back up to my curves, their coolness a shock to my skin.

He sighed while watching me, and lifted his hips off the cushion. I dropped to my knees to help him out of his pants. As I pulled them down his thighs and he stepped out of them, he looked at me with the same knowing expression from the concert.

"Suck my cock, you little thief."

God, I was wet. Everywhere. My pussy was hot and slick, and my mouth was watering. I dove onto his cock and he grabbed my head, pushing it down, and thrusting his hips up into my face. He pushed me back and knelt on the floor. I was on my hands and knees in front of him, sucking him and arching my back, forcing my ass high in the air. He let his hands roam from my hips to my head, burying himself in my throat, my nose even with his pubis. I could feel his cock pass my gag reflex, and silently congratulated myself for all that deep-throating practice I'd done in college. I swallowed around his dick, the muscles of my throat closing even more tightly around him.

His knees were wide apart, and I felt his hands on me, back, steadying his long frame. His body loomed over me and I felt tiny. How much did I want him to continue spanking me? So much. A hand moved to my ass and I flinched—tensed—thinking that he was about to smack me hard. I winced around his cock with anticipation, which I hoped sounded to Nick like fear. I hoped he thought I was afraid he might hit me again. His cock responded, jumping in my mouth. I kept sucking, back into my rhythm, and waited.

His spanks came fast and hard then, first one side and then the other, peppered with words like "slut" and "thief" and "bitch." I moaned around his cock and writhed with pleasure when he spanked me, the experience overwhelming my senses, my brain only registering thrill and pleasure when he struck me and called me names.

"You're a dirty little thief, aren't you?"

"Mmmmmmmmmm…"

"You like stealing things? This is what happens to girls who steal," he said, as a hand drew back and struck not my ass, but between my legs, sending needles of pain and searing light into my eyes. I whimpered around his cock, which was so damn hard, so big in my mouth, and I pulled off, wrapping my hand around the shaft and holding firmly. "Please," I moaned, "please fuck me."

He laughed. "Colette's such a slut. First she steals from me and then she begs me to fuck her wet pussy. I could drag you downstairs to the police right now and tell them you stole from me, but you're lucky you're so hot. I'd much rather punish you myself and then fuck you senseless." He stood up and walked to the corner. I watched on my knees as he pulled a switch from an arrangement in a tall vase on the floor before ordering me, "Come here."

I hesitated. His hands were one thing, but this? This might

be taking things too far. I might not be ready for this. He stood, waiting, looking at me expectantly and almost kindly. I gathered myself, stood, and walked over.

Nick set the switch on the back of the couch and put his arms around me. I was breathing shallowly, nervously. He kissed me. "I'm proud of you, Colette. You're very brave to be doing this, and I'm going to take care of you. I want you to stand and face the wall for your punishment."

The way he spoke made me trust him. He continued. "It will only last a little while, I promise. Then I'll fuck you like you want me to. You really are a good girl; you just need to be taught a lesson."

My pussy was swollen, my clit aching for more slaps and damn, I wanted to have him inside me. I was enjoying this game, enjoying not being the one in control of the situation. I nodded to him and walked to the wall, placing my hands above my head and spreading my legs. I took a breath and felt him move into position behind me.

"Stand still," he said. "If you move or try to get away, your punishment will be longer."

I felt the smooth, lightweight wood sliding up my leg and back down again. The hairs on my neck and arms stood on end. I trembled. I thought about bolting, grabbing my jeans and running downstairs. I thought of calling Tricia, at the very least, but I wanted to see where this would go.

I barely noticed the tapping on my right cheek; quick, light *tzt-tzt-tzt*s that became faster and covered a wider area. It didn't hurt. My ass was so hot from his slaps and my pussy was throbbing. I shivered, raising my shoulders and dropping my head back. I wanted to look at him, but I didn't.

There was a quick *whoosh*, and I heard the switch make contact with my skin. I gasped in surprise, expecting pain. There wasn't any initially. A second later I howled when it registered. Before I could catch my breath another swing came, and another. I felt like I was choking on my tongue. His hand touched my raw skin and pressed. He leaned into my ear and whispered, "Breathe."

I closed my eyes and swallowed, then slowed my breaths like we do in yoga class. My face was hot and I let my head fall forward between my arms. He readied himself again. I was prepared. I raised myself onto my toes and pushed my ass back. I knew what was coming: the other cheek.

Three strikes on the second side and I gasped with each, smiling as the pain became something better. I heard the switch fall to the floor and Nick swallowed, catching his breath. "Turn around, Colette." (Did he say "Turn around," or "Don't turn around?" My head was swimming, and I wasn't altogether certain.) I looked over my shoulder and saw him standing a few feet from me.

He'd taken off his shirt, and there was sweat on his forehead. His hands were at his sides, empty. I slowly spun to face him, bracing myself against the wall. He stepped forward and bent down to kiss my forehead, then my cheeks, and finally, my mouth. I kissed him hungrily, pulling on his lips with my tongue the way a kitten will suck on your finger if it's been weaned from its mother too soon. His cock was hard against my stomach, and he sighed when I pressed into it. "Can you stay?" he asked. I nodded and put my arms around his shoulders as he picked me up and carried me to his bedroom.

The room was dark but for a blue neon glow from outside the window. As he walked to the bed in the center of the floor, I lifted my cheek from his shoulder and smiled. With one arm holding me, he crouched down and pulled back the duvet, exposing the satiny sheets. He put me down on my knees, never taking his hands off me, and carefully avoided touching my ass, which felt like a bad sunburn. He crawled onto the mattress and eased me down. The sheets felt cool and soft beneath me, and he smoothed my hair from my eyes.

"How are you?"

"Mmm," I replied. "I'm really good. Really, really."

"I'm glad."

Nick lay on his side next to me and slowly traced his fingers over my body like a whisper. Like a feather. He did this, traveling my neck and shoulders, breasts, belly, and hips, giving me shivers and causing little gasps from my throat. Not five minutes before he'd been beating me with a stick. Now he was taking a languorous tour of my skin—this skin that he'd been abusing for his pleasure. That turned me on so much: the shift from taskmaster to lover. This change in his demeanor which, though I'd felt safe and in control the entire time we were in the living room, made me feel like a princess—like a little girl who'd been hurt and scared and needed comforting. I closed my eyes and let his hands take care of me.

His touching slid down to my mons, covering it completely with the heel of his hand, and curling his fingers down to my labia. My legs moved themselves out of the way, and I turned my head to face him, eyes still closed, a smile on my lips. He kissed me then, his lips covering mine and tugging firmly. My pussy clenched as his fingers pressed against its entrance. He pressed the tip of a finger just inside, moistening it, and drew a line up to my clit, circling it with my own juice. My back arched and I sighed.

He moved between my legs and spread my lips with his fingers. "Such a pretty pussy," he said, touching his tongue to it, "so hot and wet." I moaned and touched his hair, stroking it as his tongue and lips stroked me. *So gentle,* I thought, *so sweet.* He found my clit and, as though he could read my mind, began flicking it so quickly I thought my head would explode. Fingers were teasing my pussy and the pressure on my clit was so intense, my hips pressed up to meet his mouth, which was rolling and swirling and sucking. I didn't want to come yet; I wanted to keep feeling the warm and cool tingles alternating from my clit and the anxious feeling in the pit of my stomach that wanted release. I resisted until I couldn't wait anymore and grabbed the back of his head, pushing myself fully off the mattress, letting out a long wail as my pussy contracted around his fingers and I came.

My mouth was dry, my legs were shaking, and every breath came out as a tiny cry. When I opened my eyes, he was lying beside me. He reached over to the nightstand and opened a bottle of water. He lifted my head and held it to my lips. "Thank you," I managed. He smiled and kissed me. The glimmer in his eyes when he pulled back was becoming familiar to me. I almost asked, "What are you planning to do now?" but Nick was not as mysterious as all that. I knew the answer. Besides, his dick was hard against my leg.

He replaced the bottle on the nightstand and pulled a condom out of the drawer. I watched as he rolled it on and then rolled over me. The feeling of him pushing his cock into my pussy was thrilling, and I wrapped my legs around him as he pinned my arms out to my sides and slowly fucked me. I liked how we fit together, how his cock looked sliding in and out of me. How it seemed like his cock had been made exactly to fit my pussy. I liked how he let my arms go and balanced on his forearms and moved inside me, eventually thrusting harder and faster until he came, moaning and pumping and then stopping still to catch his breath.

I didn't say anything, just held onto his ass as he came, slowing my breathing to match his. Nick pulled out, tossed the condom in the basket, and rested his face on the pillow next to me.

He was still sleeping when I woke up at dawn. I went into the bathroom and washed my face. I caught a glimpse of my naked body in the full-length mirror on the bathroom door. I turned slightly and saw the marks on my ass: three perfectly straight lines on each cheek. Running a finger over them, I was surprised at the sting my touch produced. I crept through the bedroom and into the living room where my clothes were neatly laid on the couch.

As I pulled on my jeans, I winced, wondering how long it would take for the welts to disappear, or at least stop hurting so damn much. But I was satisfied, happy even, as I replayed the night in my mind. He had taken me by surprise, and the biggest surprise of all was how much I enjoyed it: the spanking and the sex and the way it made me feel. I was surprised at how turned on I was by his "punishment," and how much I loved the way I felt when we were fucking. I wanted more of his game. I wanted more of him.

The sun was shining through the blinds as I put on my shoes and saw a glint of metal on the coffee table. His laser. I smirked, now the mischievous one. I grabbed it like a kid collecting candy at a parade and shoved it giddily into my pocket. I scrawled my phone number on a piece of paper and placed it on the table. I walked out of the building, smiling at the cops in uniform outside the police station.

An hour later I was in my bed, the small cylinder and my cell phone on the pillow beside me. As I was drifting back to sleep, the phone beeped. I opened it to read the incoming text.

"Thief."

I smiled, sat up, and started typing.

A RARE FIND

Donna George Storey

Now Lawrence says the whole thing was my doing, but he's wrong. I know the limits of my powers.

Yes, I arranged the chairs in the living room of the cottage in a congenial circle that might be construed as a sort of theater-in-the-round. I was definitely guilty of filling the room with candlelit lanterns, the perfect lighting to bring a golden burnish to bare flesh. And I won't deny I provided several bottles of an easy-drinking Malbec that was guaranteed to loosen the inhibitions, if not the zippers, of my guests. That was all just part of being a good hostess, right?

So perhaps it was a bit provocative to show off the naughty book I'd discovered at the antique store a few miles north of our vacation retreat. But what was wrong with giving our guests something to laugh over as the evening wore on?

"*Blushing Bottoms*. You don't pass around a book with a title like that unless you're angling for something to happen," Lawrence argues.

"We met these people less than a week ago," I reply. "I didn't have the faintest idea they'd be so willing to drop their pants and whack each other's behinds."

Of course he's right that by the time Joel had Wendy bent over the footstool with her butt in the air, I didn't do anything to stop him. Because the truth is, by then I did want it to happen. I wanted to hear the smack of his palm against her runner's tight buttocks, wanted to see the blush creep over the pale, exposed skin. I wanted to watch the expression on her face, the faint grimace when she took the blow followed by a slackening of the mouth that looked like something very close to ecstasy.

Our other guests seemed equally enthralled. Charlotte's eyes twinkled like the lights on a Christmas tree as she watched, and strong, silent Curt stepped behind the armchair, probably so we couldn't see that lump in his pants. And my own husband? I didn't even have to turn in his direction to know his gaze was riveted on Wendy's naked ass and Joel's hand above it, poised to strike.

If I *had* planned it, I would have been happy with the outcome, but I was as surprised as anyone at the wild things that happened that night.

When I invited Wendy and Joel over for a glass of wine that first afternoon at the lake, I was merely trying to be friendly to our temporary neighbors. I didn't know that Joel would be so clever in the offbeat way Lawrence and I both liked or that Wendy was a wedding photographer with such amusing stories to tell about her clients. It was only natural for them to return the invitation the next day and ask the couple renting the next cottage over to join us, and before I knew it, the six of us were meeting for happy hour every evening.

Charlotte and Curt might not have been the world's most fascinating conversationalists, but they did add a certain sexual magnetism to our parties. Curt was a hunk, with pecs and delts to die for, and Charlotte was a curvy blonde straight from a men's magazine. I'm not bi, except in my fantasies, but as our gatherings continued through the week, I couldn't seem to keep my gaze from Charlotte's incredible butt. It was full and round and it jiggled ever so slightly when she walked. It didn't help matters that she favored skimpy cutoffs which showed off as much of that miraculous flesh as was legal.

My fingers itched to touch it to see if it was real.

I will confess, too, that by the time Saturday night rolled around, I'd imagined them all naked. In my lazy, summer vacation daydreams, I crept into Wendy and Joel's bedroom to spy as they fucked doggie-style: Wendy on all fours, her face contorted in a grimace of pleasure as her sinewy husband plowed into her from behind. Then I'd slip into Curt and Charlotte's bedroom to watch as she mounted him and began to ride. I pictured his big hands reaching around to cup her voluptuous ass—squeezing, squeezing—while the lather of their coupling frothed down over his balls.

But these were fantasies, not plans.

"Yes, but your fantasies have a strange way of coming true," Lawrence says. "Not that I'm complaining."

"But there's a problem with your argument, darling," I reply. "I bought the spanking book on Saturday afternoon, right before the wine party. I wouldn't have had time to plan anything."

Lawrence cocks his head, remembering, no doubt, the apple-cheeked grandma at the antique store. I was lingering over a book of racy "French" postcards when she sidled up and suggested I might find some items of interest among her collection for special clients. His jaw dropped as much as mine when she guided us into a back room, done up like a proper Victorian parlor, except for the etchings of copulating couples on the walls and the collection of vintage vibrators on the sideboard. Flustered, I reached for the bookshelf. A book seemed like the safest thing at the time.

Little did I know how wrong I was.

I pulled out a small, slim volume, the first one my fingers touched. Only then did I glance down at the faded red cover: *Blushing Bottoms*.

I felt my cheeks go hot.

Out of the corner of my eye, I noticed the shopkeeper watching me carefully. I could feel the wordless challenge in her eyes brush my flesh like a caress: *Look inside.*

I opened the cover.

The contents shouldn't have been a surprise. There were old-time engravings of mustachioed gentlemen chastising girls' plump derrieres with feather dusters and riding crops. Madams in bustles and pompadours punishing what looked like the same gentlemen, except this time their trousers were down around their knees and their buttocks bore a telltale cross-hatched flush. Soon my eyes were dancing with obscene images: cocks jutting stiffly from dark swirls of pubic hair, bosoms spilling from corsets, domineering leers and pouts of submission. I suddenly felt naughty and vaguely ashamed, as if I'd been caught peeping through a keyhole and spying a hundred years of depravity and lust. My cheeks burned hotter and my buttocks began to tingle. *Blushing Bottoms* indeed.

"This is a gem, my dear," the shopkeeper said softly. "A rare find."

I murmured a polite yes. Part of me wanted to put the book back on the shelf, but my hands gripped it possessively, as if they had a will of their own.

"I want my special things to have a good home. You strike me as a young lady who would make proper use of it. I'd be willing to give it to you at a special price."

"Buying the damned thing seemed the easiest way to get out of there," I tell Lawrence. "It's the truth."

With a nod, he grants me that point at least. "But then why were you so quick to read out the rules for that kinky game in the back?"

"I turned to that page by accident."

Lawrence gives me his Freud-says-there's-no-such-thing-as-an-accident smirk.

I've just about decided it's hopeless to argue with him anymore when he begins to recite from memory: "'Heads and Tails: a Parlor Game of Chance for Naughty Ladies and Gentlemen. Flip heads and you spank, tails you get spanked. Heads you keep your clothes on; tails you take it bare. Heads, you may use an implement like a crop or a hairbrush; tails is a naked palm. Heads and the strokes come down as lightly as a feather; tails, they come down hard. Heads you take your punishment silently; tails means begging and pleading allowed, indeed, encouraged.'"

I smile. "I see my purchase has made an impression on you. But remember, it was Joel who suggested we actually play the game."

Lawrence's smile dips into a righteous frown. "He had a good reason to spank his wife."

"Wendy was just indulging in a little nostalgia with an old flame. Joel shouldn't have been nosing around on her laptop."

"Nostalgia? Didn't Joel say the boyfriend wrote that he jerked off as he read her emails? Wendy didn't deny it either."

"Come on, it was probably Joel's fault for not appreciating her as he should have. That's why women do those things. And he's not without his sneaky side. Remember how he insisted the coin rolled under the coffee table by accident? Rather convenient that he could call heads and give the spanking no matter how it landed."

"It was simple justice. Ten strokes. One for each email."

"But he should have stopped there."

"He did. That's when Charlotte took over. Remember?"

"Yeah, and she was so drunk that she couldn't even aim."

"You definitely had me fooled when you offered to help."

"And Joel certainly wasn't expecting a swat on the ass instead. But fair's fair. He deserved it for snooping." Besides, the look on his face was priceless. For a moment I thought he was about to hit me back, but his outstretched hand curled safely into a fist at his side.

Wendy was obviously grateful for my intervention. With surprising dignity, she pulled up her pants, returned to the sofa and took a sip of her wine. Leveling her gaze at her husband, she said, "I hope you'll shut up about this now that I've been properly punished."

Joel only gave her a cool smile that didn't quite reach his eyes.

I didn't doubt she'd have to suffer more punishment before Joel was fully satisfied, but I assumed the rest of us were done with spankings for the evening.

I hadn't counted on Charlotte. Lawrence might blame me for scheming, but I'd bet she wasn't as drunk as she pretended to be when she asked, giggling, why Wendy got to have all the fun because she wanted a turn, too.

The room went silent except for the summery trill of crickets.

Curt stepped from behind the armchair and placed a territorial hand on her shoulder. Even in the flickering lantern light, I could tell his face was flushed. A quick glance downward proved my earlier hypothesis correct: the bulge in his jeans would have put a baseball bat to shame.

Charlotte looked up at him with a coy smile. "Can't I have a blushing bottom, too, sweetie? Pretty please?"

"Say yes, you idiot!"

I nearly said the words out loud, but managed to bite them back at the last minute. Would all my filthy daydreams come true right in front of my eyes? Would I get to see her ass in its naked glory, maybe even stroke the soft flesh with my fingertips, priming it for a flurry of slaps that would make it jiggle like sweet cream panna cotta?

At last Curt spoke. "All right, baby, you can have your blushing bottom. But only the girls can spank you, understood?"

"*Women,* not girls, you Neanderthal." This time I did actually say it, but softly, under my breath.

"When I heard you call him names, I knew Curt was in for it," Lawrence says with an amused smile.

"Yes. That's when I came up with the plan."

So I've finally admitted some malice aforethought, but Lawrence isn't as smug as I expected. His eyes have a faraway look, and I wonder if he's thinking of what happened next: Charlotte's woozy grin as she began to unzip her shorts, her husband grabbing her wrist to stop her.

"Keep those on," Curt snarled, with a quick glance of warning at Lawrence, then Joel. "We're done with the nudity tonight."

Curt had spent most of our earlier parties doing a creditable imitation of lawn furniture, but this spanking soiree had clearly brought out his alpha-male streak. Lawrence and Joel shifted guiltily and looked down at their shoes.

That is, until Charlotte draped herself over the footstool with a soft moan, and every eye in the room was suddenly glued to her buttcheeks, displayed before us like a birthday present.

At least mine were. How could you not stare at the ripe flesh straining against the edges of her cutoffs, the curves of her full thighs? Instinctively, my gaze shifted to her face to see if she was as turned on as I was. It was then I noticed something else. Charlotte's breasts hung over the edge of the stool, and her low-cut shirt was askew so that—intentionally or not—one stiff, rose-colored nipple had popped out for anyone to see. Beside me Lawrence swallowed, a wet, clicking sound.

Curt was apparently oblivious of his wife's secret peep show. He gave a mock bow and gestured toward Charlotte's rump. "Ladies, whenever you're ready."

I glanced over at Wendy. I could tell she didn't like the new Neanderthal Curt any more than I did. With a slight nod to me, she knelt down beside Charlotte and touched her shoulder gently. "Hey, Char, do you really want this?"

Charlotte replied with another giggle.

"It's true that it's better when 'girls' do it to you. We know all the tricks." Wendy's tone was soothing, but I sensed an undertone of mutiny. "So, first things first. Let me help you get comfortable."

She grabbed Charlotte's waistband and yanked it up so the crotch bit deep into her cleft like a thong. Charlotte wiggled like a puppy. No doubt she was getting some nice pressure on her vulva. My own pussy clenched at the thought.

Wendy began to rub Charlotte's buttocks in slow circles with her palm. It was a massage, not a spanking, but Charlotte didn't complain. She rocked her hips back and forth and let out a cooing sound.

As if on cue, Wendy gave Charlotte a swift slap on the ass.

Charlotte jerked and sighed.

"Was that too hard?"

"No, it was good," Charlotte murmured.

Wendy nodded and cupped Charlotte's right asscheek. At first I thought she was just resting, but as I looked closer, I saw that her fingers were kneading the flesh gently. Charlotte's mouth gaped and her breath came in quick gasps.

Wendy seemed to revel in the slow teasing—not just of

Charlotte, but the rest of us, gazing spellbound at the scene. It struck me that not so long before, she'd been the one with the blushing bottom, but now she held all the power in the palm of her hand.

"Wendy, honey," Curt interrupted. "It looks to me like you're enjoying this a little too much. Maybe it's time to go back to your husband for more hands-on training?"

Lawrence and Joel snickered like frat boys.

Curt turned to me. "Do you think you can do a better job?"

"I did read a book on the topic," I said sweetly.

Curt grinned back—the sucker—and stepped gallantly aside so I could take Wendy's place. Yet, once I was finally exactly where I wanted to be, I wasn't sure I could pull it off. For starters, Charlotte's musky perfume was making me dizzy and her crotch was so wet, the dark fabric glistened. Suddenly all I wanted was to lick her there, like a lollipop.

Curt cleared his throat.

Which reminded me of my true objective.

I raised my outstretched palm high over Charlotte's ass. Four pairs of eyes followed me, then paused, as I stopped in midair. I could feel the room grow hotter, fueled by the scorching glow between their legs—their cocks twitching, cunts clenching, buttocks tingling. My own body throbbed from the thrill of it. This was better than fucking someone. It was much better, because I could fuck everyone in the room with a simple flourish of my hand.

I lowered my arm to my side.

Soft groans of disappointment filled the room.

"I can't do this," I announced primly. "Charlotte doesn't deserve to be punished. She's a good girl."

"How many good girls beg for a spanking?" Curt shot back.

"She's not begging," I replied. "She hasn't said a word."

Charlotte took her cue. "Please...please spank me."

I paused, as if I were struggling with my conscience. "Why? Why do you deserve a spanking?"

"I've...been...bad," Charlotte gasped.

"What have you done that's bad?"

Charlotte wiggled her buttocks in frustration. She didn't yet realize the answers didn't matter.

I clicked my tongue. "You don't have to say it. I know what you did. You let Wendy pull your shorts up so they're rubbing against your clit. It's turning you on, isn't it, Charlotte?"

She whimpered assent.

I pulled back my hand and gave her a satisfying smack right on her tender crack. An electric jolt shot through my palm straight to my pussy. Charlotte cried out and arched her back. She was ready for more. So was I.

"There's something else that's turning you on, isn't there? You like bending over this stool and showing off your ass to men you barely know. Are you a naughty show-off, Charlotte?"

Beside me, Curt's breath was coming harsh and fast, like a bellows. It was working: I was hitting him right where it hurt.

"You don't need to answer," I purred. "Actions speak louder than words. But before I spank you again, you have to do something really bad. You have to play with the pretty pink nipple that's hanging out of your shirt. Show Joel and Lawrence how you like to be touched. Hey, even your husband might learn something. Will you do that for me?"

"Y...yes," Charlotte stuttered. Her elbow lifted as she brought her hand to her breast. My own chest tightened in anticipation. Would she really do anything I asked?

"Goddammit, that's enough."

In a swift move, Curt knocked me over so I toppled back against Joel's legs. He grabbed Charlotte's arm, pulled her to her feet, and stuffed her naked breast back into her shirt. His chest was heaving and his face was brick red. I'd even bet his bottom was blushing, too. And it was all my doing. That much I wouldn't deny.

Curt couldn't resist a parting shot, however. He jerked his chin toward Lawrence and snarled, "Hey, mister, you'd better learn how to keep your wife in line." Then he hooked his arm around Charlotte's waist and shoved her out the door.

Lawrence helped me to my feet.

Joel waited until their footsteps had faded to quip, "What do you bet he fucks her in the woods before they get fifty feet from the porch?"

We all laughed, but a question still hovered in the air. All the ordinary boundaries between us had been slapped away—what came next?

Wendy reached for her husband's arm. "It was a great show, folks, but I'm afraid we have to be going now. Joel has to fuck me in the woods on the way back."

Smirking mischievously, they left Lawrence and me alone to face each other in the flickering lantern light.

Lawrence smiled. "I have to say, you know how to throw an interesting party."

"Lucky for you, you don't know how to keep your wife in line," I replied saucily.

His eyebrows lifted. "On the contrary, I think you might need a firmer hand. Especially tonight."

Given the events of the evening, I should have been prepared for this, but the remark was so unlike Lawrence, I tilted my head in confusion.

"Come on, you know exactly what I'm talking about. Now take down your shorts and bend over the stool."

His voice was calm, even playful, but my stomach tightened

—with fear or arousal, I wasn't sure. Still, you could say I had it coming to me. Hands trembling, I unzipped my shorts.

"Keep the panties on," Lawrence added. "But take off your shirt and bra. And make sure your tits are hanging down over the stool, just like Charlotte's."

Now the tingling sensation had settled between my legs—and it was definitely arousal. As I leaned over the footstool, I realized my pussy juice was oozing down my thighs.

Lawrence knelt beside me. "The problem is you fell a little short in your duties as hostess tonight. You did a good job of whetting our appetites, but you didn't give us the main course. Now I want some meat."

He hooked his fingers on each side of my panties and tugged them up tight into my crack. My tender flesh throbbed, just shy of pain, but now I understood why Charlotte had wiggled so deliciously. Soon I made another discovery: when I pushed my pelvis against the edge of the stool, it put pressure on my clit that felt like I was masturbating. No wonder Wendy had worn such a look of saintly ecstasy.

"You were so clever, so much in control," Lawrence continued in his avuncular tone, "but I'll bet you secretly wanted to bend over and get your ass spanked, too."

"Yes, I did," I confessed, my voice faint with lust.

"So tell me what you have to do to deserve it."

"Play with my nipples?"

Lawrence chuckled. "That's exactly right. You must read books about these things. Shall we get started?"

I brought my trembling hands to my breasts. They felt swollen and tender, and my nipples were already hard when I began to flick them with the pads of my thumbs. I hardly had a chance to sigh at the pleasure of it before Lawrence landed several blows on my exposed rump. The heat rippled through my cunt, which caused the muscles to spasm so hard, I thought I might come on the spot.

"I'm already close, Lawrence," I begged. "Will you fuck me now? I want the meat, too."

He didn't answer for what seemed like an eternity. I thought he meant to tease me for a good while longer, but then I heard him fumble with his zipper, felt his fingers pull the drenched string of my panties away from my hole. With no further preliminaries, he plunged in to the hilt, and another gush of juices glazed my thighs as he jammed against my swollen G-spot. Then he began to move, our bodies making rude slurping sounds as he pumped in and out. Each thrust brought an extra gift: a smack on my asscheeks, first the right, then the left. His blows were measured, even encouraging, like a jockey urging his prize filly to the finish line, each stroke bringing me closer and closer, until my orgasm galloped up through my throat in a whinny of victory. A few seconds later, Lawrence emptied his balls into me—bellowing loud enough that if our guests were still fucking in the woods, they would have known exactly what we were up to as well.

"All right, maybe you didn't plan the whole thing from the beginning," Lawrence says. He's tired of arguing, I can tell. "But you have to admit the old lady at the antique store was right. You did make good use of that dirty book."

I smile. "Oh, no, I haven't even started. There are a lot more amusing things in it for us to try. But I will agree with the old dame that it was a rare find."

"No, you're the rare find." He grins, eyes twinkling, and I know he'll play right along with all my naughty games and enjoy every minute.

Which, I'll confess, is exactly what I'd planned from the beginning.

GAME, SET, MATCH

Sage Vivant

Declan had finished the round robin match with the other boys, as Thelma liked to call his friends, and now settled in to watch his wife finish her match.

He was not at all impatient for the ladies to finish. Each of them looked downright delectable in their tennis dresses and skirts, and he never tired of watching them. Selma and Rochelle, both nearly six feet tall with legs born to be flaunted, often teamed up with Thelma and Barbara for their weekly tennis games. Selma and Rochelle had instructed their husbands to stay away from the tennis club when they played—they wanted them to perform the dirtiest household chores so that when they returned from a rousing tennis match, they'd be greeted by a sparkling house. Declan had never met their husbands, but knowing what he did about Selma and Rochelle, he imagined they scrubbed floors and toilets without complaint. A strong woman was a commodity worth washing and waxing for.

Barbara, his former fiancée, cut a striking figure, as always,

with her athletic gait and abundant confidence. Since his marriage
to Thelma, he tried not to recall the heady discipline sessions at
Barbara's knee, but sometimes he couldn't help himself.

Nobody, however, stirred his mind, body, and soul like
Thelma. Even as he watched her move about the tennis court
with the grace of a gazelle, he vividly recalled being draped over
her lap to receive her blows. He adored her without reservation
and let pride wash over him as he settled in as a spectator for the
last few minutes of their game.

Two young couples were talking behind him—they were
waiting for their turn on the court. Declan realized that the
women were running a bit late and so he waved to them. Thelma
waved back, but appeared oblivious to the time.

He turned around to face the young people. Introductions
were exchanged.

"You'll have to forgive the ladies on the court," Declan
explained. "Once they get going, they lose track of time."

"Oh, it's okay. We're a bit early," said the taller thirty-some-
thing man whose trophy wife had a glazed and sullen look that
didn't seem to lend itself well to tennis.

"I'm sure they'll be finished soon. You know how it is with
us older folks—we need to be reminded about everything!" He
chuckled and they joined in politely.

"Speak for yourself, Declan. All of us were very much aware
of the time," Thelma said from a place very close to him.

When he turned around to face the court again, all four
women were glaring at him. Sparks barely contained themselves in Thelma's eyes, and Barbara's nose practically expelled
smoke.

"Oh, there you are!" He tried to sound relieved and even
pleased to see them, but his temples felt like a tennis racket
in play.

"Yes, here we are. Right on time," Thelma snarled. "How dare you characterize us as feeble old women?" She spoke softly but the young couples surely heard every word.

"Oh, we didn't take it that way!" the young man said in Declan's defense. "He only meant that—"

"I think his wife knows what he meant," Barbara shot back. "Don't you have a game to play?"

"Oh, sure. Yes. Well. Okay. Thanks," the man muttered and helped to usher his fellow players to the court the women had recently vacated.

"You know, Thelma, this is what happens when you give them privileges," Barbara pointed out. "He played tennis with the boys and now he's cocky."

"I'm outraged, Declan. Absolutely outraged," Thelma said, still keeping her voice low and steady. She pulled out a chair from the round table, laid her racket down, and eased herself into the chair. Her lap beckoned. The other women were quiet now, watching just how Thelma would deal with her errant husband.

"Take your position, Declan. I will not tolerate being belittled in public without showing you how it feels."

The four young people had already started their game and had forgotten about the mature group of women. Declan dared not look to one side or the other to determine who else might be watching. Thelma wouldn't like that.

"Get up, she said," Barbara interjected.

"I can handle this, Barbara," Thelma told her.

Head spinning, Declan managed to get to his feet, whereupon Thelma told him to drop his drawers. He let his outer shorts fall to the cement, did not step out of them, and approached her in his briefs with tiny steps. When he assumed his place across her lap, his cock immediately pushed itself against her thigh. He hoped she would not take offense.

She ignored his hardness. Instead, she yanked his briefs down to expose his helpless derriere. He caught a glimpse of Thelma, whose tight lips were pressed together in a self-righteous grimace. He returned his gaze to the ground before him but from the corner of his eye, he saw her reach into her bag under the table. From it she extracted a mahogany hairbrush nearly identical to the one she kept at home. He wanted to smile at her highly developed flea market shopping skills, but just as quickly as the thought occurred to him, it disappeared—the hairbrush met his naked skin in one swift wallop.

He panicked as much as he thrilled. What if one of his tennis buddies saw him in this position? What if the tennis club's management took issue with this sort of public spectacle? Declan was willing to subject himself to any punishment Thelma might deem necessary for him, but he didn't want their "regular" lives affected by their dominant/submissive one. But he had to trust that Thelma used good judgment. That was his job as a submissive.

The sting of that first stroke of the hairbrush turned out to be a mere introduction to what lay in store for him. Thelma spanked him relentlessly, ignoring his wails, impervious to his pleas. His tears flowed into her warm, voluptuous lap, which he surreptitiously licked in gratitude. He kicked and squirmed to no avail—Thelma did not stop applying her hairbrush to his behind until she determined he'd received his due.

"Enough," she announced, returning the brush to her bag. "We don't have time to continue this here. You'll be caned when we get home." She gently returned his briefs to his raw and reddened cheeks, covering him with a sweet, maternal gesture that assured him of her love. The ladies dispersed quietly, leaving him alone with his dearest Thelma.

They drove home in silence, which only made Declan concentrate more on the pain emanating from his sore bum. He followed her into the house and stood in the entryway while she got a glass of water from the kitchen. What lay in store for him next? He dared not imagine, for she was sure to surprise him.

"How are you feeling?" she asked him in between long swigs of her water. Despite his pain, he was able to appreciate how fetching she looked in her tennis dress.

"I feel very chastised, ma'am."

She smiled. "And we aren't even finished. What you got at the tennis club was for the public embarrassment you caused me. What you're about to get now is just general punishment. You should have known better than to misbehave as you did today, Declan."

"Yes, ma'am. I was very foolish. I wasn't thinking."

"No, you weren't." She downed the rest of the water in her glass. "Prepare for twelve strokes of the cane. Go up to the guest room and wait."

He obeyed and waited in the guest room for what seemed an exceptionally long time. He heard her moving about the house, lingering in the bedroom doing something that made considerable noise. Was she moving furniture without his help?

She opened the door to the guest room, wearing an elegant silver caftan with a prominent necklace. "Come to the bedroom now, Declan."

In the bedroom, she'd moved her vanity table to the middle of the room and attached her best down pillows to the top of it with rope. "Lie down on that," she commanded. She stared at him, which told him that he was responsible for removing his clothing from the waist down. The height of the table with the pillows caused just his toes to touch the carpet as his legs hung over the vanity. She moved his hands so they clutched the outer edges of the vanity table, and then showed him the old English school cane that she'd be using to deliver his punishment. It was a formidable instrument, and he trembled just thinking about all the little English arses it had branded in its lifetime.

The first swat was naturally the most intense. His bottom, still very sore from the hairbrush that morning, experienced the focused landing of the cane as a sharp electric current that traveled quickly down his legs.

"One," Thelma counted with a purr in her voice.

Thwap! "Two!"

And with each point of contact, his thoughts became more addled. He could no longer think clearly—all that existed was her voice, counting, and his pain, radiating. He wept and cried out but as usual, it was to no avail.

"Eleven," he heard in the distance, uncertain whether he'd already received the eleventh whack or if it was soon to follow. He'd lost count of the blows.

"You've been so naughty," Thelma said, positioning herself so that her luscious lap rested against his head. She stood before him but because of his subservient position, he could not see above her thighs. But now that his head was nestled between her legs, he could smell the familiar aroma of her pussy. He was so hard he could barely breathe.

"Are you wondering whether I've delivered twelve strokes yet? You've lost count, haven't you?" He whimpered that he had. "You'll get number twelve when I feel you're good and ready for it," she told him. "Unless you tell me that you want it. Do you want it?"

"Yes, ma'am, I want the rest of my spanking. Oh, please. Give me my twelfth stroke!"

She said nothing, didn't even move. Was she angry? Had he said the wrong thing? How could he rectify whatever error he'd made? Without warning, the final stroke of the cane descended on his fiery rear end and he called out for the last time, bawling like a colicky baby.

"Go to bed, Declan. Think about what a bad boy you've been," she said.

She left the room before he did to give him one smidgeon of dignity. He stood on wobbly legs, watching the room spin as he tried to stay upright. The raw, throbbing pain at his backside made it difficult to put one foot in front of the other. He touched himself where the cane had been and counted twelve individual welts. *Imagine the attention to detail Thelma must have employed*, he thought to himself, *to leave each mark so I could identify it later*. Eventually, though, he stumbled out of the room and into their conjugal bed, where cool and silky satin sheets awaited his burning, spent body.

He longed to rest, even to sleep, to regain his strength, but his sobbing kept him awake. His remorse vied with his pain to make sleep elusive. Just as he floated toward some sort of oblivion that resembled sleep, however, Thelma entered the bedroom. He was facing the door and saw her come in. She wore the same caftan and jewelry that she had when she'd caned him. Her hair framed her face in waves that softened her beauty and reminded Declan of a goddess.

She seemed to float toward him in her luxurious caftan. When she was next to the bed, she slipped the garment over her head to reveal her naked, breathtaking curves. She kissed his forehead, caressed his ear, and got into bed beside him. In total silence, she held him like the baby that he was. Her warm skin pressed against his stirred him and made sleep completely out of the question now.

After a few moments of spooning to reestablish their bond of intimacy, she crawled on top of him, straddling his hips. The warmth from between her legs made his pubic area prickle with sweat—his or hers? No matter, he enjoyed it either way.

"Rub my clit for me, sweetheart."

The moment he touched her wetness, her aroma permeated the room. She was juicier than any young woman could have been, and his fingers were coated with her cream in seconds. She gyrated her hips to indicate that he needed to syncopate his rhythm with hers. He complied eagerly.

The heat from her sopping wet vortex increased, as did the size of her beautiful clit. He had no sooner forgotten about the lingering pain at his rump when across the threshold stepped Barbara adorned in...absolutely nothing at all.

Her sizeable breasts swayed as she approached the bed. Thelma looked over at her without surprise, so Declan understood that she'd invited her to join them. He found the turn of events far from objectionable.

"Barbara is going to sit on your face, sweetheart. I want you to eat her out until she's come as many times as she wants," Thelma explained.

Barbara looked a bit smug but in the bedroom's dim light, Declan could easily choose not to see it. She knelt on the bed at first and just kissed him. He continued to finger Thelma while he kissed Barbara, but he understood that Barbara's tenderness, communicated through her long, sensual kiss, was meant to disarm him and make him trust her. Because Thelma had invited her, he had no qualms about trusting her—Thelma would never put him in a position where he would be hurt.

Just as he prepared himself to diddle Barbara in the manner by which he was pleasing Thelma, Barbara broke away from their kiss and mounted his face. Her scent, deeper and muskier than Thelma's, had been lost to memory since their separation years ago, but its familiarity came rushing back to him now as it filled his nostrils. The folds of her labia caressed his nose and lips until his tongue squirreled into her slippery hole.

And so he coaxed one wet pussy with his fingers and another with his mouth. Both women practically gushed with amorous enthusiasm. His efforts were beginning to pay off, however— both clits were tighter and harder than they had been. Thelma came first, exclaiming a throaty appreciation for what his fingers had wrought. He loved the feeling of her writhing in his hand, and it was all the more exciting because Barbara blocked his view of her, so he could only imagine the way she looked as she trembled her way through her orgasm.

When she was finished, she immediately impaled herself on his now pulsating cock. She guided him into her swiftly and efficiently—the way she did everything. Once he was firmly inside, she rode him hard and fast, slamming her body down on his hips to force his meat deep inside. Her strong legs clamped against his hips, another reminder that she was the one in control.

Just as his balls started to tighten, Barbara erupted into her own private pleasure party. She ejaculated slightly, sending an extra shot of wetness over his face. He continued to lap away at her, as per Thelma's instructions, and spasm after spasm, he never stopped pushing her to new heights. Her orgasms were as difficult to count as they were to measure, so he didn't try. He only let her scent, her moisture, and her moans guide him. She never seemed to tire of grinding her mound into his face, sometimes even depriving him of air. Sometimes, she'd bounce, other times she'd slide seductively over his nose or chin. Through it all, he never stopped licking whatever part of her nether regions she pushed at him.

One grand shout seemed to punctuate the conclusion of her steady stream of pleasure. When she slipped off his face, she edged backward toward Thelma, who held her upright by taking hold of her breasts. The sight threatened to relieve Declan of every drop of semen, but still he held out—he hadn't been given permission to come.

"Barbara and I both like it from behind," Thelma said as she fondled Barbara's breasts. Both women were looking down at him. The persistent angle of his cock was not specifically addressed but it sat inside Thelma in a highly agitated state.

"Then I will take you both from behind, ma'am," Declan said, glad his voice sounded stronger than he felt.

The women climbed off him and positioned themselves on hands and knees as Declan sat up and prepared to fulfill their wish. Their exquisitely round behinds were so fetching, upturned and eager as they were for his cock. He had paused, wondering which of them should be first, when Thelma relieved his confusion by talking over her shoulder to give him instructions.

"Insert yourself into Barbara but finger me while you pump her," she said.

Barbara's warm, tight entry, still creamy from the orgasms he'd just given her, pulled him deep inside her. His fingers pushed gently into Thelma's juiciness, lingering over slippery folds and puffiness. He forced his mind to think about sports or needlepoint or car repair—anything not to indulge in the enticements that surrounded his cock and smeared his fingers. He could not give Barbara what he knew he must save for Thelma. He just couldn't. But if Thelma didn't allow him to get inside her soon, he would be filling Barbara with ejaculate he'd been saving up for hours.

"Fuck me, Declan. Fuck me now," Thelma growled.

He didn't want to seem too eager to pull out of Barbara—she might get angry that his desire for both women wasn't equal—so he did his best to make it appear that he was reluctant to leave the incredible heat of her hole. Once he was out, though, he caressed one of her asscheeks while he shoved himself hard into Thelma.

"May I come inside you, ma'am?" he asked, hoping that his question would force her to answer not only the when but the where of his inquiry.

"No, you may not," Thelma said between grunts as she met his thrusts with her own. "When you're ready, spray us both."

Her request was not difficult to fulfill. In less than six seconds, he was holding his slick penis and pointing it at their backs, watching as prodigious ropes of sperm decorated the women's backsides. They wiggled and squirmed as it landed on them, a charming sight that he'd commit to memory for quite some time. Just as he remembered that he needed to clean them up with some sort of towel, they moved so that they were upright, backs facing each other. He watched as they pressed their backs against each other and slid up, down, and sideways to work his semen into their skin.

"That was lovely, Declan," Thelma said to him while her breasts jiggled with her movements against Barbara. "In fact, it was so nice that I'm going to invite Barbara to join us once a week. You won't know which day she'll be here, though—it will vary from week to week. But you must be ready to please us both, just as you did today."

"Or you'll feel the wrath of our punishment," Barbara purred, winking at him.

"Yes, ma'am. I understand and I'm happy to provide whatever either of you might need. It will be my pleasure to do so."

"Very good, dear. Now go to the kitchen and make us some snacks. We've worked up quite an appetite," Thelma told him, just before she kissed him long and hard on the mouth.

TIED DOWN

Andy Ohio

I was a little embarrassed to talk about my problem. Fortunately the saleswoman was not only knowledgeable but tactful as well. "A lot of our customers have that problem, especially in New York. The walls aren't strong enough to support eyehooks or pulleys. In cases such as yours, I would suggest an Under the Bed Restraint System," she said, and pulled out a plastic box with Velcro cuffs and a complicated system of nylon webbing. "It's not as complicated as it looks," she continued. "You put the nylon webbing under the mattress so that there are cuffs at each corner of the bed. All the straps are adjustable so you can restrain someone pretty securely. Also, the cuffs hide under the mattress easily, so you only have to pull it out discreetly when you're ready."

I looked at the picture on the box. "But the restraints are Velcro. Aren't they easy to slip out of?"

She handed me one to try. "Feel that. They're secure. And if your partner can't reach one hand with the other, they're not going anywhere."

I was sold. I bought it, took it home, set it up, and texted Helena: *Be at my place at 10 p.m. I'm going to tie you up, whip your ass, and fuck you.*

I suppose this could use some explanation.

Helena was a tall, beautiful, leggy blonde that I'd met a few years previously when I worked in advertising. She was a shark with a ditzy demeanor and infectious giggle that belied her keen intelligence and business savvy—a modern-day Judy Holliday in Jenna Elfman's body. We had stayed in touch after I quit advertising and more than once she had called me up at the last minute to help her on a project that was headed for disaster.

A few weeks earlier, I had saved her once again, and she took me out to dinner as thanks. Dinner turned to drinks, which turned to a night on the town that ended up with us back at my place smoking pot. "I'm not very good at it; you'll have to help me," she said, handing me the pipe. "Can you blow the smoke in my mouth?" I leaned in with a mouthful of smoke, and we started kissing. Soon we were naked on my couch, fucking. And I mean fucking—hair-pulling, dirty-talking, sweaty, nasty, *fucking*.

We moved from the couch to the bed, and I bent Helena over and slipped in from behind. Holding on to her hips, I furiously pushed myself into her and pulled myself out, then paused and slapped her ass hard. Helena moaned and I did it again, leaving a red handprint. She moaned even louder. I slapped her again even harder then leaned over and whispered in her ear. "Is that okay?" I asked.

"Yes," she said. I pulled out, and I started to spank her with full force. Her ass got bright red, and she moaned more. "You like that?" I hissed at her. "You like that, you fucking whore?"

"Yes!" she moaned as I continued to spank her until she started to cry. She was only crying softly, but I didn't want to go any further.

We lay down on the bed, and I held her close with her head on my chest, stroking her hair, and whispering to her, "It's okay, it's okay, you're such a good girl. You know I'd never hurt you for real, it's okay. Are you okay?"

She looked up at me, her eyes shiny with tears, her nose red from sniffling, her hair tucked behind her ears, and said, "Yes, I'm better than okay, I'm fantastic," and then kissed me deeply, pulling me on top of and into her. My cock was harder than I could remember it being since I was a teenager, and I came inside her with startling intensity. Something, or someone, inside me had woken up.

Until I met Sigmund, I was a bottom. Sigmund was studying to be a psychologist. He was also very masculine and good looking, with a swimmer's body and hairy chest. He worked out every day and was into extreme sports and had a huge cock that I quickly decided was not going anywhere near my ass. "That's okay," he said, "I like getting fucked." During all my years as a practicing homosexual, I had never topped anybody; I had never felt up to it. All my fantasies and scenes had been about submission and subterfuge, about placing the responsibility with someone else. But I really liked Sigmund, and he really wanted me to, so one night in bed, I turned him over and started to fuck him in the ass, and it was great. That was the moment where everything started to change. I started to look at the world—and my life—differently. I felt in control, and I started making changes.

The next time few times I saw Helena we had great sex, with no spanking, no humiliation, and no dirty talk. Then one night, we were coming back from a party and started making out in the cab. I don't know if it was something we ate, but we got so worked up that we barely made it back to my apartment. I opened the door and as soon as it closed I started pulling off her clothes. With her dress and panties around her ankles, I pushed her up against the wall and started kissing her neck and rubbing her breasts. I took off my belt just to get my pants off and then started to rub it over and into her pussy until both the belt and my hand were wet. I could smell leather and sex as I folded my belt in half and, holding Helena's wrists together in front of her, whipped her ass once with it. She gasped sharply and then moaned. "Is this okay?" I asked.

"Yes," she said, and I did it again.

"You like that, don't you, you little slut?"

"Yes."

"Yes, what?"

"Yes, sir."

I whipped her with my belt again and again asked, "You like that, don't you? You liked it at the party when all the men were coming on to you? You dreamed of getting fucked, didn't you? You nasty fucking whore, you like getting your ass whipped and getting your pussy fucked? I know you do because your pussy is so fucking wet." I kept whipping her with my belt, not so hard that it left marks, but firmly enough that it made a loud slap, enough for me to know it stung.

Helena was moaning and shouting, "Yes!" until all of a sudden she wasn't, all of a sudden she was crying, really crying. This time it was deep sobs, heavy, like a dam bursting. I immediately stopped and took her in my arms, held her tightly, and led her to the bed. It was like flicking a switch that changed me from Nasty Dom Top to Sensitive Jewish Guy.

"Are you okay?"

"Yes, I'm fine. I don't know why I'm crying," she said through her tears.

"It's okay, it's okay. You know I'd never really hurt you. I care about you. It's okay. Listen, don't worry, just let it out, let it out."

I held her close, murmuring in her ear, calming her down, comforting her. "Shh…" I whispered, taking her chin in my hand and looking into her eyes. "You know you can trust me, right? You know I'd never hurt you for real, right?"

"Yes, I know," she said. I looked at her tear-streaked face and soft mouth, her lips gently parted. She looked so beautiful, so vulnerable and open, I looked at her wide eyes and nearly fell in.

The next night we went out to dinner and, over some wine, I asked her about it.

"Helena, what were you crying about; did I hurt you?"

"No. I don't know what it was all about. I guess I was just drunk and weepy. I wish you hadn't seen me like that."

"Don't think that—listen, with my history, I don't judge anybody. You can be whoever you want to be with me, do what you want to do, really."

"I know, but…"

"Listen, do you want me to stop being kinky with you?"

"No. I like it."

"Because I have to be honest, I like it, too. It's kind of a new thing. I never really knew I liked it, but it is amazing. It makes me feel so close to you. I love it, I guess, because it's like you're in trouble and then I…"

"Get to save me?"

"Yeah, save you, exactly."

"Do you know how many times you've already saved me? Either at work or by talking to me when I'm freaked out?"

"Yeah, I guess so. It's heavy. I mean, emotionally it's intense."

"I like it. Don't stop saving me."

From there the sex—and the emotions—started to get deeper and more complicated. I had always been more amused at the leather/BDSM scene than anything else. My friends and I would go laugh at the men at Folsom Street East with their inch-long nipples and their "slaves" in gimp masks and on leashes. I had been to fetish parties but found it hard to take seriously—all these people adorned in leather and latex seemed to be more on display than anything else. I would watch the scenes, but the dialogue always seemed poorly scripted and empty. Now it was different. Now I started to understand. I have always been jealous; I have always had trouble expressing anger, always been afraid of losing control. But with Helena, I found myself listening to these emotions and channeling them into our sex play. Sometimes I would find myself hoping she'd do something to make me angry, just so I'd have an excuse to discipline her. Once she showed up to meet me an hour late and as high as a kite, wearing fuck-me pumps. That earned her a major spanking and bent-over-the-chair fucking.

Another time she picked a fight in a restaurant. She was angry about work, she was angry with herself, she was tying herself in knots, and taking it out on me. I paid the check and left, saying, "I don't need this shit."

Four hours later I was in bed, reading, when she texted me. "I'm sorry for being so vile." I turned off my phone and started to go to sleep. My landline rang. "Please, please, let me come over. I'm sorry, can I please come over?"

"Fine, use your key to let yourself in," I said and rolled back over.

I was half-asleep when she took off her clothes and got into bed with me. "I'm so sorry. I don't know why I picked a fight with you. It's just...it's just what I do."

Fine. Whatever. "Let's talk about it in the morning."

She was still crying as she held me, threw a leg over my waist, and offered her ass. "I'm sorry," she said, "I don't know why I do it..."

"You're sorry? You think you're sorry? You think you're

crying now? Well, wait until I'm done with you." And I started to spank her ass, hard. "You think that's fucking funny? You think I like listening to you argue with me? Throw a fucking hissy fit at me? That's bullshit!" I kept smacking her. I was really angry and really turned on.

"I'm sorry, I'm sorry," she said. "I don't know how I can make it up to you."

"I don't know either, but you can start by sucking my cock, you pain in the ass little slut." I grabbed her hair and put her head on my dick, forcing it in deep. "Suck that fucking cock, you nasty cock-hungry whore!"

I really, honestly, hadn't known I could say things like that. It was exciting, and it was terrifying. I have a secret personal history of violence, and I felt like I was flirting with something dangerous.

"Listen," I said the next day. "I want to talk to you."

Helena looked at me. "What's up?"

"I love what we're doing, but I'm getting confused. I'm having a hard time telling where the truth ends and the play-acting begins."

She sat there, sphinxlike.

"Sometimes we act like a regular couple and do normal couple-y things; sometimes we have really fun, playful sex. And then sometimes we get into this other thing. And I really like it but sometimes it feels like all this is, is sex."

"I don't want to label this or put it in a box, Andy."

Now I was the girl.

"I understand that, that's cool. But I feel a lot for you. I think we have strong emotions for each other, and every time it starts to get serious we…"

"Look, I'm just not comfortable with labeling what we're doing. Come on, let's go fuck."

"No, I don't think so. I need a night off."

We took the night off. We took two nights off, and all I could think of was Helena in chains. And then it was Sunday, and I was walking past a trendy sex store, where I stopped in and bought the Under the Bed Restraints. I texted Helena, ran some more errands, and went home to wait.

Ten p.m. and Helena showed up.

"Take off your clothes and get on the bed," I said.

She lay down and we started making out. I pulled her arms up by her head and pinned her down. Using one forearm, I kept her under me as I reached for a cuff with the other hand. Once her right hand had been secured, I reached over and cuffed her left, kissing her the whole time. I tightened the straps, got up, and cuffed her feet. I looked down at her splayed naked on the bed, her long body beautiful and restrained, her blonde hair spread around on the mattress like a golden penumbra. I started to kiss her on the mouth and worked my way down, sucking on her nipples, licking her pussy. I worked my way back up, pinching her nipples, flicking them with my tongue till they were hard. I reached under the bed and told her, "This might hurt; let me know if it's too much," as I put a clothespin on each nipple.

Helena moaned, "Oww..." I asked if it was too much. She sucked in her breath sharply and exhaled, "No," between clenched teeth. Good.

"Good girl."

I pulled out my dick and rubbed it across her lips. She struggled against the restraints but to no avail. I grabbed her head and held it as she took my cock in her mouth. I thrust in and out, reached over, twisted the clothespins. I reached a hand down and worked two fingers into her pussy, keeping pressure on her nipples. I took my dick out of her mouth and my hand off of her pussy and reached under the bed, taking out a black vibrator and easing it in. I repositioned myself and started to work the vibrator in and out of her cunt as I licked and bit her clitoris. I could feel her struggle, and I lifted my head to look at her face contorted with pleasure, her muscles straining against the straps. I kept fucking her with the vibrator and taking her clit in my mouth, every once in a while switching positions to tweak her nipples. Her moans turned to screams. "Oh, god! Oh, god! No, stop! It's too much!"

I stood up, pulled the vibrator out and took the clothespins off of her nipples. I looked down at her, watched her adjust, listened to her catch her breath. As she lay there panting, I took off the rest of my clothes and climbed in between her legs. I looked down at her looking up at me. I put a few pillows under her ass and started to fuck her, hard. I could feel her under me, trying to move, trying to break free. She moaned and I kissed her to shut her up. She was bucking against me as I forced myself into her. I felt incredibly powerful and incredibly close. She looked at me, a little bit afraid and a lot turned on. Our bodies were covered in sweat. I pulled out and released the cuff on one leg, crossing it over the other so I could reach her ass. I started to spank her ass with one hand, holding her free ankle down with the other while I stuck my cock back in and started fucking her again. Her ass started to glow red as I spanked it, hard. The sound my hand made as it struck her was crisp and sharp.

Finally I couldn't take it anymore. I pulled out and came all over her face. I stepped back to look at what I'd done. She was tied down and covered in sweat, her face flushed, her skin blotchy and red. She was panting and exhausted and grinning from ear to ear. I leaned in and gave her a kiss, tasting myself in her mouth. I undid one cuffed hand and then the other, then got up and undid the remaining bound ankle.

I pulled her onto my lap and spanked her one more time. She

moaned. I spanked her again. I put two fingers in her cunt and started to fuck her with one hand while I spanked her harder with the other. She was bucking wildly against my hand when she howled, and I felt a gush of liquid all over my hand. "Oh, god!" she cried.

"Are you okay?" I asked.

"I'm better than okay," she purred. "I'm fantastic!"

Then Helena scrambled out of my lap, put the pillows back at the head of the bed, lay down, and pulled the covers around her.

"Come here," she said. "Let's go to bed."

THROUGH A GLASS, SHARPLY

Elizabeth Coldwell

Elliott is in the living room, waiting for me.

I sent him there a good fifteen minutes ago, more than enough time for me to have cleared away the dinner plates and stowed the leftovers in the fridge, and he knows it. But I told him I would be in when I'm good and ready, and perhaps I'm just not ready yet. I know he will wait patiently, however long I take. At the moment, I'm sitting here, finishing off a glass of chenin blanc, and listening to Fauré's *Requiem*, letting him stew for a little longer, to allow the feelings of anticipation and excitement to churn in his stomach, just the way he likes it.

Mind you, he could have been anticipating exactly this scene for longer than I thought. I certainly had no thoughts of punishing him this evening—after all, I spent most of the afternoon preparing rack of lamb in a rosemary crust and white chocolate and raspberry brûlée, and when I'm struggling to follow a recipe, I have no thoughts of dishing out pain to anyone, unless it's the chef who blithely presumes the average home cook shares his level of expertise with a boning knife. However, at some point during the evening our eyes met and a look flashed between us, some unspoken signal which indicated that both of us were up for a spot of fun. Perhaps it was having to listen to Elliott's boss, Mr. Wilkins, as he told us all about his recent golfing holiday in La Manga, including an excruciatingly detailed account of his hole in one on the thirteenth. Perhaps it was the teeth-grinding effort of making conversation with his snobby, opinionated wife, whose specialist subject was the enormous profit they had made on selling their home, and how they had downsized at just the right time, with the property market certain to implode in the coming weeks. Perhaps Elliott appreciated just how much work I had put into making this evening a success, and realized that I needed to let off steam. Whatever it was, we both knew that at some point we had to wreck comprehensively—even if only in private—my husband's image as ideal senior management material.

Of course, Elliott had to find some excuse to be punished— neither of us would gain any enjoyment if I were to spank him without cause—and it was halfway through the main course that he reached out to refill Mrs. Wilkins's glass and, somehow, sent it clattering, splashing its contents across the table. He was considerate enough to make sure it was white wine he was spilling, not red—which would have meant a liberal scattering of salt to mop up the stain, followed by the quick whisking away of the table-cloth, rather than a little mopping and a lot of apologies—but in that moment of carefully calculated clumsiness, he had done enough to ensure that I would be warming his bottom later on.

The final, ethereal strains of the *In Paradisium* fade away to nothing, and my wineglass is empty. I feel centered, relaxed, and ready. I click off the CD player and put the glass in the sink. I smile to myself, wondering what Elliott's boss and his wife would say if they knew that, now that they are safely on their way back to Muswell Hill and the dishes are sloshing in the dishwasher, I am going to spank my husband. Even if they were aware that we played these kinky little games for our pleasure, they would assume I was the one on the receiving end. After all, in his sober Savile Row suit, with his hair that is conspicuously graying even though he's barely into his thirties, and his deep, commanding voice, Elliott appears to be the perfect dominant. Whereas I am almost a foot shorter than him, petite and blonde and something of a scatterbrain, and seemingly designed to be hauled over his knee to squeal and wriggle beautifully as he turns my bottom a blushing crimson. But appearances can deceive: my husband is no stern daddy, looking for a daughter figure to discipline, and I am no rebellious brat who needs to be tamed. Knowing that our true natures confound everyone's expectations simply adds an extra, delicious depth to my husband's willing submission and my enjoyment of it.

Even though he has been expecting it, Elliott still starts guiltily as the door opens and I step into the living room. He is waiting in the position I requested, the position I always request: standing facing into the corner with his hands clasped behind his back, thinking on what he has done. Though he'd removed his jacket and loosened his tie over the course of dinner, I told him to put them back on properly: stripping my husband out of his formal work attire is all part of the pleasure of the scene for me. You have never really known power until the man you love is at your feet, naked or very nearly so, helpless and vulnerable, while you remain fully dressed and completely in control.

I go to stand close to him. We never adopt roles during a spanking—it seems unnecessarily artificial to both of us, and I would feel foolish, somehow, pretending to be the strict school-mistress or the authoritarian boss. Elliott knows from the tone of my voice and my body language that from now until his punishment is over, I dictate what happens, and that is enough for me.

"So," I say. "Have you had enough time to think about what you did?"

"I think so, ma'am," Elliott replies hesitantly.

"You understand why I am so displeased with you?"

"Yes, ma'am. You set the table so beautifully, and I made a mess of the tablecloth."

"And that glass was part of the set my brother brought back from Venice for our wedding present. It's very precious to me. What would you have done if you had broken it?"

Elliott is not one of those annoyingly manipulative bottoms who will deliberately break something of value in order to add extra venom to a punishment. However, he was taking a risk by playing with that glass, and I need to make him aware of it. He pauses for a moment before replying, "I would do whatever it took to find a replacement, ma'am. And whatever it took to make you happy."

"I'll tell you what would make me happy." My voice is soft, so that he has to stoop slightly to hear me. As I speak, I run my hand over the front of his trousers, feeling the hard length of his cock rising up toward his belly. I suspect he has been hard from the moment he knocked over that glass of wine. "Turning that backside of yours scarlet with the flat of my palm. Take off your shoes, socks, and jacket and pull down your trousers, Elliott. Then bend over the back of the armchair."

Elliott hurries to obey. We have a leather-backed armchair in the room that would be more fitting for a Victorian gentleman's study than our modern, minimally decorated home, but it has pride of place because it is always the centerpiece of our punishment scenes. I watch as my husband takes off his jacket, folds it, and lays it on the seat of the chair. His shoes and socks follow, discarded socks tucked into shoes, shoes pushed under the chair, out of sight. Then he unbuckles his belt and lets his trousers fall to his knees. As he bends over the chair, the tails of his crisp white shirt partly conceal his firm buttocks. I come up behind him and tuck them back on themselves, then run my hand gently over his bottom, stroking it through the clinging cotton jersey of his underwear.

"What a beautiful arse," I tell him, and I mean it. It's a part of his body I would love even if I didn't have any interest in spanking it, muscular from the hours he spends in the gym and the Sunday morning football kickabouts he enjoys with his friends. "But it needs to be taught a lesson. This arse needs to know that when the boss is round for dinner, we all have to be on our best behavior."

By the end of the sentence, my gentle caresses have become firm taps. Not enough to make Elliott flinch, but enough to begin the process of warming up his bottom, ready for the harder blows to come.

"Yes, ma'am, I'll remember that in future," Elliott says. And then he doesn't say anything for a while, as I begin the process of spanking him in earnest. My hand comes down on his buttocks over and over, sharp little slaps paced so that he never knows quite how long he will have to wait before the next one comes down. He can take a lot of punishment, particularly when I'm using my hand, instead of my hairbrush or the doubled-over length of his belt, and he squirms slightly but I know I'm not really hurting him.

After a few moments, I reach for the waistband of his underwear and begin to pull it down.

"No, ma'am," he murmurs, a little halfheartedly, "please don't take those off."

"Why not? Why shouldn't I bare your disobedient arse? Is it

because you know that I'll discover this—" And I reach round between his legs and take hold of his cock. The smacking I have already given him has done nothing to diminish the strength of his erection. The tip of it is already wet with his excitement, and he feels hot and alive in my palm. I tug at him a few times, just enough to hear his breath start to quicken. It wouldn't take much to make him lose control, but I don't want that to happen just yet. Not when that gorgeous arse of his is so rudely exposed to me, begging to be beaten.

"Oh, bad Elliott." I sigh. "Bad, bad boy to get so turned on. Are you enjoying what I'm doing to you?"

"Yes, ma'am. Please don't stop, ma'am."

"What, don't stop wanking you—or don't stop smacking your arse?"

"Both, ma'am. They both feel so good."

"Do they?" This time when I bring my hand down on his backside, it's with just about all the force I can muster. A few of these blows are guaranteed to leave my own palm stinging, never mind my husband's flesh, but now I've raised the stakes it won't take long to carry this through to its inevitable conclusion. A couple of spanks, then I teasingly run my fingers along the length of his cock. A couple more, and I pause to cup his balls in my hand, finding them ripe and ready for release.

The final hard volley of slaps is punctuated by my sharp words. "Will you do this again? Are you sorry? And will you obey me in future?" He gives all the right answers, even though I know it won't be too long before he gives me another excuse to have him like this, his bottom rosy and tender from the impact of my slaps.

"Stand up," I order him. He does as he is told, legs slightly shaky. His cock is bobbing up in front of him, desperate for relief. I don't even give him a moment to regain his composure before I say, "Make yourself come." As I watch, he grasps his cock in one hand, balls in the other, and begins to wank himself. He looks so beautiful, naked apart from his shirt and tie, the dynamic young executive reduced to a humble penitent who will do anything I desire. It only takes a few swift tugs before he is coming, his seed oozing out over his rapidly pumping fist.

He sags back against the armchair. "Did that please you, ma'am?" he asks, when he is able to speak again. It's his standard question after a punishment; he always needs the reassurance that I am satisfied with his performance.

"It did, but don't think you've finished pleasing me yet. Come into the bedroom," I order him, picturing him crouching on the bed, lapping at my suddenly needy pussy. "I have an idea of how you can make it up to me for spilling that wine...."

REUNION

Madlyn March

Shouldn't she be in prison by now?" Darlene asked, looking over my shoulder.

I followed her gaze and my eyes fell upon Toni Aniello, the tomboy who made high school hell for me. Yes, I know every kid gets bullied, but trust me: I had it worse than most. Toni pulled my hair, beat me up, banged my locker door against my hands, told on me to teachers when I did nothing wrong, and stole my most prized possession: my autographed picture of Nancy McKeon from "The Facts of Life." To answer your first question: no, I didn't know I was gay back then. To answer your second: yes, I know I should have.

"She hasn't changed all that much," Darlene said.

"No," I remarked, as I watched Toni awkwardly bopping around to Bananarama. "Twenty years later and she still can't dance worth shit."

"Still has the mullet," Darlene noted.

"And still thinks flannel is appropriate formal wear," I added, laughing.

Before you yell at me, yes, I know we were being mean. But I think I get a free pass on this one, as Toni had terrorized me for years and, I was sure, never felt the slightest bit of remorse over it. Just between you and me, I admired her for that. I often wished I was more like her because then I wouldn't have been such a victim. But, alas, my mother had handicapped me by giving me a conscience.

Standing there, staring at Toni, I suddenly had an urge to grab her by the bottom of that mullet and drag her down into the punch bowl. It was good to know I hadn't matured over the past two decades.

"Do you remember how she got in between you and Lena?" Darlene asked.

I felt my heart flutter. "I'm not discussing Lena."

Lena, who was pretending I didn't exist while she stood by a wall with some jerky-looking guy, was my very straight, very platonic high school sweetheart. Every confused gay girl has to have one. It's practically a requirement of being queer. Ask your lesbian friends. Buy them some drinks, and they'll regale you with tales of tortured "romantic friendships" that left them with more evenings of blue clit than they'd care to remember.

Lena was a real winner—a girl who could have given Catherine Zeta-Jones a run for her money in the looks department—what with her jade green eyes, glossy black hair, and ridiculously adult cleavage. She was also bright and more than a little bit mischievous, just the way I like my women. In two weeks, she and I became best friends. We were together so much my brother once asked if we even shit together. A classy kind of guy, my brother is.

Anyway, that all changed when Toni started chatting Lena

up. I don't know what she told Lena, but I know Lena never spoke to me again. It took four more years and a woman built like Pamela Anderson before I could properly recover.

Was Toni hot for Lena? I never knew. Toni was one of those girls everyone suspected of being gay, but she still went out with the boys. Maybe they were covers. Or maybe she was fool enough to think she really was straight. Last I heard, she'd even had a serious college boyfriend. Poor sucker.

"She's staring right at you," Darlene said.

Darlene was correct. Toni was staring straight at me, and smiling, as if to rub the whole Lena thing in my face again.

I downed the last of my martini and nudged Darlene. "Come on. Let's go," I said. "I've had enough of this bullshit."

"Hey," Toni called from across the room.

"Just keep walking," I said to Darlene. "Ignore her."

"Hey!" she yelled louder.

"One foot in front of the other," I said.

"Hey!"

"We better stop," Darlene said.

"Hey, Elizabeth. Is that you?" Toni asked. Now, she was right in front of us.

"Yep," I said. "It's me."

"You aren't leaving, are you?"

"I'm afraid I am," I said.

"Well, don't go just yet," Toni said. "We haven't even gotten to talk." She was smiling. I realized I was now five inches taller than her. This reassured me, but only slightly. I wondered if I could take her down, all these years later. I'd certainly love to try, but we both had crow's feet and some gray hair. It wouldn't be the most age-appropriate thing to do.

"I have to get back," I said. "I have—"

"Kids?" Toni asked.

"No."

"A husband?"

"No," I said, trying not to burst out laughing.

"A dog?"

"No. Well, not since Banjo died."

"Good," she said cheerfully. "Well, I mean, not about Banjo, but good that you have no reason for going right now. I have something I want to talk to you about."

"I-I don't know."

"Come on, I won't keep you long."

Before I could protest, she put one arm around me and we started walking. Darlene didn't even look back at me as she raced toward the exit. Lucky bitch.

"So, Elizabeth, I want to apologize." Toni's breath smelled of gin. Apparently, she needed liquor to be remorseful. At least this explained why she couldn't be nice to me when we were younger.

"You don't need to apologize," I said, even though she'd done enough damage that now my therapist could afford that second house in the Hamptons. "Bygones," I said, waving my hand.

Toni laughed. "Well, that was easier than I thought it'd be."

"Why? Did you think I'd burn you at the stake?" I asked, then pictured doing just that.

"No. But I did think you'd get a little angrier."

"Anger solves nothing," I said.

"How very Deepak Chopra of you," Toni said while massaging my neck.

Truth was—and I would have died before admitting this out loud—she was pretty darn cute. Sure, she had the bad hair and even worse fashion sense, but she was quite the handsome little butch. And I was quite the horny little femme.

"Uh, what are you doing?" I asked.

"You seem stressed out. I can sense the tension from here. I know; I do this for a living."

Now, *there* was irony. Hands that had once caused me pain were apparently now giving others pleasure. That God has quite a sense of humor on him.

I looked around, worried that someone would see us. My high school class was a pretty conservative bunch, and I was sure at least one right-wing nutcase would object to two middle-aged dykes engaging in foreplay, even though it was of the PG-13 variety. But no one said a thing. I guess they were, like us, three sheets to the wind.

Toni kept massaging my neck, but suddenly it felt like she was massaging my clit. Good lord, how long had it been since a woman last touched me?

Actually, it had been four years. My last lover, Mimi, was fun, but frustrating. She loved to spank me, which was a problem, as I prefer being the spanker. We didn't break up over that, but it made the sex—at least for me—much less satisfying than it could have been.

"I was so cruel to you when we were kids," Toni was saying. "I deserve to be punished for what I've done, don't you think?"

"Uh-huh," I said, grabbing a mini–hot dog from a tray. I tried not to think about what it looked like as I shoved it in my mouth. "And just what kind of punishment were you counting on?"

She leaned in closer and whispered, "One that involves my bare ass and your cruel hand."

"Uh-huh," I said again, nervously gulping my fifth martini. "So you're into that kind of stuff?"

"Yeah, and by the look in your eyes, I'd say you were too, Little Miss Not So Innocent. Tell me. Do you like to give spankings, Elizabeth? To horny butch women?"

I couldn't even speak at this point. I settled for rapid nodding.

"Good. I know where we can go so you can give me all the punishment I need."

She grabbed my hand and we walked away from the tacky streamers, the deflated balloons, the disco ball, the dashed dreams. She took me to a quiet spot outside.

"We could get caught," I said.

"Makes it all the more exciting," she said. "So, how shall I worship you this evening?"

I almost burst out laughing.

At that moment, I realized I was in control of the unlikeliest bottom in history.

I could really play this to the hilt, I thought. I mean, what better way to make Toni pay for her past crimes than by being her master? I could take revenge for my high school self and get some pussy at the same time. A perfect evening, all around.

I noticed her undoing her pants. I put a hand over her zipper. No, no. She wasn't getting off that easy. Literally.

"You're not ready to undress yet. You'll undo your pants when I say you can. You made my life miserable, Toni Aniello," I said haughtily, like some actress from a John Waters film, "and now you'll pay."

Toni whimpered, loving every minute of it.

"Yes, Elizabeth," she said.

I slapped her hand. "And don't give me that Elizabeth shit. It's Mistress Elizabeth to you."

Toni's eyes grew wide. She smiled. I smiled, too. Then I frowned.

"Get that smile off your face," I said, pushing her against a tree. "Or else I'll wipe it off for you." God, but I was rusty in the dominatrix dialogue department.

While she stood there, I wrapped one arm around her waist and put the other down her pants. I fingered her cunt, torturing her until she was begging for release. Then I took out my hand and put it to my own cunt to give myself some much-needed relief.

"All right," I said, a few minutes later. "I think you're ready for what I have to give you next." She dutifully unzipped her pants. "Lie back on the ground," I said as I rummaged though my bag, wondering what I could use to restrain her and to hit her. Ah. Perfect.

"Ass up," I said, as I pulled her hands back with my ponytail holder.

I hesitated for a second. Was this right? Would I hurt her too much? It seemed strange to care, considering what she had done to me. But she seemed like such a nice person now, and I didn't want to do anything that would be too—

"I bet you still hate me for taking Lena from you, huh?" she asked.

Suddenly, I stopped caring about whether what I was doing was right or not. She obviously wanted me to be rough. There was no other reason why she'd bring Lena up after all this time. She was trying to make me as mad as possible so I'd hit her hard. God, she must be dying for a good spanking. Well, she would just have to wait. Wait and suffer.

"No, I don't hate you for taking Lena," I lied, gently massaging her bare ass with the back of my metal hairbrush. "But I bet you wish I did. I bet you'd like to feel the sting of this. It'll really hurt when it hits that ass of yours. I'll whack you so hard, your clit will feel the vibration for days."

She was breathing loudly. So was I. We were frozen like that for two whole minutes, both terrified and excited by what was to follow.

Then I made good on my promise. Hard.

"Unngghh," she groaned.

I stuck my fingers under my panties and began fingering

myself. When I felt she could take a second hit, I whacked her even harder. And again. And again. The hardest metal hitting the softest skin. Over and over. After each whack, I touched my clit, taking myself just to the edge but not over. I whacked her until those pale globes turned bright red. I whacked her until I was almost ready to come myself. I wanted to put myself in the same place she was: Dying to have an orgasm, but not wanting to end the exquisite torture. Not yet, anyway.

I remembered how it felt when Mimi did it to me. At first, you're surprised someone's hitting you, even if you've asked her to. Then you're excited. Then you're in pain, but it's a fantastic kind of pain. Each slap makes you want more, as much as you can take, until you can't take any more, and you're shaking, more than ready to have an orgasm, the kind that can only be gotten from a woman diving headfirst into you with her wet tongue licking rapidly.

By this point, Toni was moaning and crying. I started to panic.

"Toni," I said, breaking character. "Are you okay?"

"No," she said, looking up at me. "I'm better than okay. Please. Whatever you do, don't stop." She touched my hand, and silently pleaded with her eyes.

The transfer of power was complete. She was in my control.

I continued smacking her, alternating the brush with my hand. I dug my long nails deep into her round cheeks after each satisfying whack, making it hurt just a little bit more.

I paused to feel the results of my hard work. Just as I expected. Her ass felt fiery and her cunt was dripping. I played with her pleasure button just a little bit, teasing her.

"Please," she said. "I need to come, Elizabeth. I mean, Mistress."

"No," I said. "Not yet."

Before, I had been using just the front of my hand. Now I realized I could do a much better job with the back. I undid her restraint and told her to put that lovely red ass across my lap.

I put all the strength I had into that last spanking. I spanked and thought of how Toni and I felt so much self-hatred about being gay that we had to punish ourselves by chasing a girl we knew we could never have. I spanked and thought of all the fun we'd missed out on, fighting when we should have been going out with each other.

I stopped and noticed a small tree branch.

I hit her with it, knowing that the twigs would further sting her already bruised behind, like pouring salt into the wound.

Finally, without telling her, I went back to my bag and searched for my vibe. Yes, I carry one around. Doesn't everyone?

First, I pleasured myself as she watched. I had restrained her again so she was unable to do a damn thing about it but squirm. I felt wonderful as I dropped my pants and put my own bare ass up to the breeze. I positioned my wet cunt over the vibrator and felt the most glorious orgasm overtake me. I even allowed myself to get a little dramatic—groaning loudly—just so Toni would suffer some more, watching me.

Finally, I stood and pressed the toy against her clit, holding her tightly as she came. And boy, did she come. I worried our whole graduating class could hear. But as much as she'd enjoyed herself, she also seemed strangely unsatisfied. I could see yearning in her eyes as she finished that last glorious wave. So I smacked her some more with my brush. That did the trick. Each smack only seemed to make her hornier. The harder I slapped, the harder she pushed that greedy cunt of hers against my vibe. At the end, I took off the restraint and licked her clit and watched as her whole body vibrated with pleasure.

When she was done, we just sat there for a while, staring

ahead. Adam Ant played somewhere in the distance. I felt myself coming back to reality.

"Lena liked you better, you know," Toni said. "I was just jealous. That's why I took her away. It's why I bullied you so much too. I-I'm sorry, Elizabeth." She started to cry. "I'm so sorry. You didn't deserve it. I've felt guilty about it for all these years. It's the only reason I came here tonight. I had to apologize."

"It's okay, Toni," I said, as I rubbed her inflamed and beautiful behind. "I think we're more than even now."

RIDING
THE STORM

Thomas Christopher

Standing in the hayloft of the old gray barn, I looked out the open hay shoot and watched the bruised blue storm coming toward us over the mountains. Lightning from deep inside the storm sent white light bursting like flashbulbs against the dark clouds. For a moment I wondered what my wife and Julia's husband were doing at the campsite up in the mountains. No doubt they were huddled in the tent, prepared for the storm, and wondering what had happened to us hiking in the valley.

I was wondering what happened myself when I looked down again at Julia's smiling face. Her playful tongue flicked and swirled and slid around me. The delicious teasing made me jerk and jump, causing her to smile even more, before she took me into her mouth completely. My head fell back from the sudden jolt of pleasure, and I caught a glimpse of the huge beam running along the peak of the barn's roof above me, before I closed my eyes. I thought I was going to come, but then Julia pushed me away, and I almost fell over on my ass. She laughed like it was the funniest thing she had ever seen.

She jumped to her feet—I'd never seen her so giddy and girlish before—and she slithered out of her snug hiking shorts and kicked them up in the air. Thunder kept rumbling with muffled booms that echoed in the valley, and lightning snapped against the mountains with a sound like breaking twigs. The wind blew harder, and it felt cool against my hot, sweaty skin. Julia twirled around to face the roiling storm clouds outside and jutted her magnificently round ass at me like it was a gift.

"Spank me," she said. She dropped to her knees and then onto all fours, her head down and her ass high, wriggling her butt like she couldn't wait. "Spank me like a bad girl, a dirty girl, a filthy girl who sucks the cock of her friend's husband."

Her ripe bottom in that submissive position, burning to feel the sting of my hand against her raw flesh, inflamed me in an unspeakable way. I was finally going to spank that wonderful plump ass that I'd been lusting for ever since we answered the ad looking for a fun young couple to go on weekend hiking and camping trips with. From the first time I saw her curvy behind squeezed into a pair of tight hiking shorts that cupped each bubble cheek like the skin on two juicy apples, I wanted to pepper her ass red with loud, hard smacks and bury my cock between her luscious cheeks.

Only two weeks ago, when we all drank too much after hiking all day, the conversation somehow turned to the topic of sex. Julia confessed that she had a boyfriend in college who was obsessed with her ass. He loved to indulge his fascination by standing her up naked against a wall with her hands over her head and blistering her butt with a paddle until he become so aroused that he'd grab her violently, throw her down on the bed, and drill his cock into her asshole. She described it more delicately and less profanely than that, but essentially that's what she said. Her husband said he'd never heard that before, and my wife looked away; however, I made a point of catching Julia's eye and letting her know I wished I'd been that college boy and gotten to be the lucky one beating her ass, whipping us both up into an unbelievable height of sexual ecstasy that would have reached a peak when we fucked each other to blinding orgasms and then collapsed into a wet pile of satisfied flesh.

I knelt beside her and banged my knees on the rough wood floor, feeling the stab of the sharp splinters, but I didn't care. I could barely control myself. Being this close to her without spanking her furiously and devouring her thick lush ass took all my strength. Unable to resist smacking her, trembling with the need, really, I whacked her panty-covered ass with a quick, jarring strike to calm my excitement and let her know I was going to enjoy every minute of this. She jerked forward when I hit her, her ass flinched, and she let out a breathy "Oh" before settling into her submissive position again: head down, ass up.

"Lie flat," I said.

She obeyed, and I drank in the sumptuous sight of her white panties and how the fabric stuck deep between the twin mounds of her cheeks. I followed the thin black line the panties made curving down into the wet shadows between her legs. I groped her sweat-dampened underwear and breathed in her salty sweet scent. Then I drove my teeth into her tender flesh to take a bite. She screamed and then laughed. But I wanted more. So I gripped the waistband of her panties and tore them off, elated to see a snow white bottom, made all the more brilliant against her tanned legs, and I was even more elated to see the far white cheek stained red from my first slap.

She wiggled her ass, making it jiggle. She loved this. My cock stiffened. She said, "Please, spank me. Please. You're killing me." She turned her head and looked up at me with a naked craving in her eyes, her lips still shiny wet from sucking and slurping my cock.

With her eyes still on me, I raised my hand back like a whip. She stared at my hand held high. I kept it there a moment, poised to strike her at any second, making her wait for it, building the anticipation, making her want it even more, making her yearn and ache with desire for that beautiful sting on her bare ass, waiting and waiting until she couldn't take it anymore, her mind going dizzy. I wanted to hear her plead, desperate and whining. I wanted her on the verge of shuddering, her cunt tingling and dripping, so that when the blow finally came, when it finally landed, it would send her mind and body reeling.

"Do it," she said. "Do it. Stop torturing me. Do it. Spank me. Please, please, spank me. I need it. I want it. Please, give it to me. Do it now. Oh, god, do it. I can't take it anymore."

Her ass shook and squirmed below me, like she was trying to shake free from tight ropes coiled around her. I aimed for her blushed cheek that I'd struck the first time. I brought my hand down, swinging it hard enough that I felt the strain in my shoulder and my elbow, my arm snaking into a lash that snapped against her ass with a sensation and sound that nearly overpowered me. The heat from her flesh flared up into my hand. She cried out at the painful sting. Her ass quivered and rippled from the blow. I savored the feel of her soft ass flattened by the stroke of my hand. An electric shiver went through my body. I slipped my fingers between her thighs to see how excited she was. Her cunt was overflowing, juicy like an overripe melon, and I squished my fingers around, wallowing in it, until they were soaked. Then I made her suck the juices off, swirling my fingers around her hungry tongue as she hummed with pleasure.

But there was more spanking to be done, and I quickly

slapped my wet fingers against the fresh snow of her unstained cheek. I held my hand down tight to admire the pressed flesh and feel how my hand sunk in and formed a deep valley before I let go and her butt burst back into trembling shape. My nerves tingled at seeing the new red mark of my handprint blazing on her white ass.

"You don't know how much I've wanted this," she said. "Please don't stop. Spank me. I'm yours. You own me. Spank me more."

Before she had barely finished her words, I spanked her again, feeling the blood in my cock pulse hotter. Julia twitched her ass with glee and arched it up with thrilled anticipation for the next blow, tightening just before my hand hit her again. I squeezed, clutched, grabbed, and twisted her beautiful plump ass as if it were mounds of decadent desserts and I wanted to stuff fistfuls of it in my greedy mouth.

That did it. Crazed to stain every inch of those white cheeks crimson, I struck blow after blow against her flaming bottom. Julia writhed and thrashed under the barrage of spankings, crying in sobs and yelps, but never once rolling away, not even an inch, from the next smack. She gave herself fully to the sweet torment she was reveling in. Her white ass was splattered red. I whacked her all over: on the crest of each plump cheek, along her round hips, and down her thighs, loving the sensual, smoldering feel of her doughy bottom giving way and bouncing back after each hard smack. I slapped the lower curves of her ass with a sweeping motion to make her whole bottom wobble. Her flesh rolled and shimmied and vibrated like the wind twisting on water, waves and ripples rubbing together. The endless smacks rang out against the storm, against the booming thunder and the cracks of the lightning, that all mingled into a syncopated rhythm like the throbbing percussion of a jungle tribe. The hayloft shrunk into darkness. Lightning flashed the dark like strobe lights. Black shadows shimmered and swayed. Her red ass glowed. I was out of my mind.

I tore her asscheeks apart, plunged my face into her deep crease, and drilled my tongue into her tight asshole. Julia squealed and pushed up her butt to meet my ravenous tongue. I shoved three fingers up her sloppy wet cunt and spun them around and around and in and out. She grabbed her ass and pulled it apart even harder, the rim rising and stretching so I could circle and go deeper. She dug her fingers in more, as if she were trying to open it wide enough for me to get my whole mouth inside it. I lapped and bit and tongue-fucked her tight wet hole while her fingers sank down to dance with my tongue and push at her anus, making it open, until Julia slipped a finger in her asshole and I licked around it, feeling the rim squeeze tight, feeling the ridge made by her sunken finger. It was more than I could take.

I plunged my cock into her asshole, slamming my pelvis against her burning rump, diving deep, as if I wanted to be consumed, holding it there, deep, deeper, so I could feel the tight darkness suck me in and swallow me. Then I pulled my cock out, and I flipped her over on her back and grabbed hold of her face with both my hands and buried my tongue in her mouth. Our teeth clicked. My tongue darted around inside like a snake on fire, her lips twisting with mine, our mouths inhaling each other's breaths. I drove my arms around her, scraping my fore-arms against the splintery wood floor, and I squeezed her to me with such force that she gasped. I squeezed harder, wanting to burst through her skin and become one boiling mass of endless pleasure with her. My cock plunged into her like a pillar of rock hurtling deeper and faster into thicker and thicker water, as if the ocean depths were a bottomless swamp that I was driving down so far into I was never coming back again. Her sopping wet cunt squished up and down the length of my cock, clinging to me; her arms and legs cinched around me like ropes, like she wanted to suffocate me; she was screaming and moaning with abandon. And I never wanted to emerge from it, never wanted to come out, never wanted to surface from the torrent, the flood, the deluge that was sweeping us away.

Afterward, I kissed her sore red bottom and cradled her in my arms. Lightning crisscrossed the dark churning sky like blue veins beneath the skin. Rain began to hit the barn. Thunder boomed and lightning cracked. The barn seemed to creak and sway as if it were an old ship being tossed on stormy seas. A chilly mist blew in from the hay shoot and stuck to our sweaty skin. Rain beat on the roof like rocks. We looked at each other and laughed because we both were thinking the exact same thing. The rain was blowing in the shoot like a squall, and we stretched out on our backs near the edge and let the gushing rain wash over us, beating against our faces and filling our open mouths to overflowing, until our naked bodies were drenched. We stayed there, side by side, until the storm was nothing but a distant murmur and the sun glowed orange over the ragged mountaintops.

THE BREEDING BARN

L. Elise Bland

Party at the Breeding Barn! the invitation read. When I first got the notice for the prestigious dairy farm's cocktail party, I hesitated. Would there actually be animals wandering around doing weird things? Was this an event that required rubber work boots or could I wear nice pumps? And how could I enjoy champagne and hors d'oeuvres in such a smelly place?

Curiosity got the best of me, so I RSVPed and headed up to Vermont. Since I wasn't sure what to expect, I wore a pair of high-heeled yet sturdy leather boots and a slim black pencil skirt, plus my trademark string of pearls.

Much to my relief, the dairy barn wasn't in use anymore for breeding—at least not that anyone would speak of! It was the sexiest barn I had ever seen and definitely had fucking potential. From the outside, it looked like a regular old barn, but on the inside, there were vaulted cathedral ceilings that reached into the heavens and peaked into ornate windowpanes. They let in just enough sunset so that everyone at the party looked golden.

Professional servers and caterers—both male and female—were dashing every which way in their starched white shirts, bow ties, and neat black pants. Most carried silver trays of goodies, but one guy in particular had something even more interesting to offer. Instead of the usual round tray, he had a long and very suggestive "serving board." If it hadn't had food sitting on it, I would have sworn it was a paddle. It was at least two feet long and shellacked so heavily that it glistened under the light. It even had a handle with a loop of leather dangling from the hole so that it could easily hang on the wall of a kitchen—or bedroom. As soon as I spotted his big serving board, I knew it would eventually end up in my hand, and I would be the one doing the serving.

He approached me first. It was, after all, his job to bring around appetizers to all the guests. "Would you like a baby stuffed with fresh chèvre?" he asked me.

"A baby? No thanks."

"I'm sorry," he said laughing. "I meant a baby potato stuffed with goat cheese." I didn't know if it was a slip of the tongue or an odd breeding barn joke. I just wrote it off as Vermont humor.

"Sure, why not?" I plucked one tiny potato off the board and took a bite. The empty space that my potato left behind revealed even more of the wood that I so longed for. It was truly a magnificent paddle, and the man wasn't so bad either. I soon found out his name was Josh. He didn't tell me much else about himself, but I gathered from his grooming that he was a bit of a pretty boy—sleek body, fake tan, plucked brows, bleached teeth, and moussed-up hair. My concerns were the usual: Was he straight? Would he let me spank and paddle him? And could I get a free toy out of it?

"So where did you get this cheese board?" I asked him. "It's really nice. I'm always in the market for more, especially really long ones like yours." I ran my hand underneath the board, letting my fingers slide up to the handle. He was gripping it as firmly as he would his own cock. I cupped my hand under his and gave it a squeeze. I wondered how big his cock was. I also wondered how big that cheese board handle was.

I'll admit I'm a size queen—a greedy gourmand for paddles, and the bigger, the better. I especially love scary frat boy types because they make men so nervous. However, some of the most exciting toys are those I find in the everyday kitchen—wooden spoons, spatulas, Japanese rice cake molds, pizza servers, breadboards, and ice-cold marble rolling pins to cool off a pair of hot buns after a good waling. Still, the handiest paddle of all is the human hand. You never leave home without it, and it never raises eyebrows in public.

"I don't know where they get these boards," he told me. "They have more back in the kitchen. If you want, I can let you go back there and ask my boss who makes them."

"Okay, sure," I said and followed him into a harshly lit kitchen, all the while watching his tight cheeks stretching the material of his slacks with each step. He had one of those high-riding muscular asses that I just love to get my hands on.

We bypassed the loud caterers in white chef's coats and went straight to the manager's office. The manager wasn't in, but Josh rummaged around until he found a catalog for the boards.

"Here, you can look through this and see if you like any of them." He laid the brochure on the desk in front of me. I leaned over to peruse the goods, trying to match the board sitting on the desk with the pictures in the book. Josh just looked over my shoulder at first, but soon I felt his arm touch mine. And then his chest was against my back. And then his hard cock was rubbing on my asscheeks. Finally, he ran his hand up the back slit of my skirt and pulled the material up to my hips. I wasn't wearing any panties, and we both knew how wet I was. He gave my ass a light swat.

"What are you doing?" I asked him, pushing him away, but partly wishing I hadn't.

"I'm sorry. I thought this was what you wanted. I mean, the way you were stroking my hand out there, I just figured…actually I figured you wanted to be either fucked or spanked or both."

"Well, you thought wrong," I said. "I had plans to spank you instead! But I'll settle for a consolation prize of a free paddle. Let's just call it a night." I pulled my skirt back down, grabbed the board of potatoes, and headed for the door.

When I started to turn the knob, I had a change of heart—or pussy. I pressed my thumb into the lock button and turned back around to face Josh. With my fist firmly gripped on the serving board, I flung the goat cheese potatoes across the room and walked toward him with the now dangerous implement.

"Let's make a deal," I said. "If I bend you, you can bend me. That means if you can take what I have to dish out with this appetizer board, then you can have dessert—on me."

He got the picture. I grabbed the thick hair at the crown of his head and lowered him into proper spanking position over the desk. His sturdy arms quivered as I adjusted their width.

"Stay just like that," I ordered.

From behind, I unbuckled his belt and unzipped his pants. His cock was sticking out so far that, even though it was strapped down by his underwear, I had trouble getting his slacks to come down. His tight boxer briefs proved an even greater challenge. Once he was finally exposed, I had before me a pair of perfectly sculpted cheeks and a cock with skin so taut, I almost took pity on him and gave him a hand job. But teasing sounded like much more fun. I ran my hand up the shaft and swirled it around his cockhead, which was shining from excitement. He moaned and I felt him tense up, ready to come, so I stopped. We weren't done yet. In fact, we hadn't even begun.

I swatted his butt until my palm was nice and toasty, but why waste a good hard-on? Women who prefer their guys "over-the-knee" know that a well-positioned cock in the lap makes the spanking even better.

"I want to sit in the boss's seat," I told him as I steadied the rolling chair. "On your knees, now. Crawl to me." I sat back and spread my legs slightly so that my skirt rode high up my thighs. He knelt down on the floor, trying to dodge the cheese and potatoes I had thrown everywhere. Once he reached the chair, he rolled it against the wall and buried his head in between my knees, first licking just above my boots and then along my inner thighs, so lightly it tickled. At last he found my pussy and knew exactly what to do. He drove his tongue into my lips and then slinked up to my clit, where he practically sucked the life out of me. All I could feel was his wet heat and pure muscle working every part of my cunt. The wobbly office chair jostled me into a debilitating orgasm. I was pure jelly, but I still had work to do. I had to stay strong.

"Are you trying to get out of your spanking?" I asked him afterward. "Get up here and lie over my lap now, and I want your cock sitting right where I can feel it. You know what I mean."

One orgasm is never enough for me. It's just a warm-up, so I prefer to stay high on the roller coaster and get in as many screams as possible. I pulled him over my lap with his beautiful tanned cheeks laid out before me as if on a platter.

"Cock between my legs," I instructed. I repositioned him until I had his member rubbing right on my still-throbbing pussy. I gave him a couple of love pats just to warm him up. He was so tan, it was hard to see how much color he was getting, but the heat rising from his skin told me he felt it. However, I like to spank much, much harder. I reared back and doled out a hefty blow, letting my hand bounce off his muscular cheeks. Beneath a flurry of swats, he tensed and released, and with each jump, his cock rubbed just close enough to my clit to make me want to spank more.

I thought about punishing him, but then I realized I really wasn't in the mood to invent a punishment scenario with a stranger. (Most men just inherently need to be punished for something anyway, so a spanking is always in order!) I decided to give him a pop quiz instead.

"So how many goat cheese potatoes were on my serving board?" I asked.

"I don't know. The chefs set the boards up."

"Okay, do you want me to open that door now and ask the chefs how many?"

"No! Are you crazy?"

"Well, give me a number. I know how many were on there. If you guess right, I'll give you that many spanks and you're off the hook. If you guess wrong, then you take the correct number from both my hand and the paddle." His head turned side to side, trying to count the potatoes on the floor, but it was hopeless. They had rolled everywhere, and some were even mashed into the carpet.

"Fourteen?" he asked nervously.

"No, wrong! Just as I suspected. You were just out there looking pretty and not paying attention. There were, in fact, seventeen hors d'oeuvres on the plate—after I ate the one. Do you realize what this means?"

"No."

"Seventeen hard spanks followed by seventeen blows with the paddle."

Over my knee, I led him through the series of hand swats. Some were bouncy and some stingy, while others came with a full follow-through that dug deep into the muscles. I even gave him a couple of double-handed drum beatings—two cheeks for the price of one. He was great over my knee. His cock jolted against my thighs and pussy, and his cheeks burned under my feminine touch, but I couldn't wait to try out the paddle board.

I stood him up and positioned him back over the desk.

"Are you ready to count?" I asked.

"Yes, ma'am," he said. He had finally figured out his role in the game. I grasped the handle of my glimmering new paddle and pulled back. It was mine at last, and he was mine, too, at least for the moment.

"Brace yourself, boy," I said and swung the board onto the nice soft fleshy bottom part of his cheeks—the sweet spot, as they call it. The paddle only bounced a little, but it was still a hefty blow for such a pretty boy.

"Ow," was all he had to say. I paced around the office for added suspense.

"Sixteen more to go," I warned him, twisting the door handle so it unlocked. "And each one will get harder than the last. If you can't take it, I'll open this door right now and you are free to go, pants or not."

"I'll try," he mumbled, so I locked the door back in place.

What I promised, I delivered, plus one for good measure. He yelped and squirmed. Luckily the kitchen was noisy with the usual screaming and banging of pots, so nobody heard our slaps and moans. His cheeks deepened into shades of bronze and rose with crimson speckles.

"You realize this serving board is mine now," I said once

I was done. "Now that it's had your ass sweat on it, it's been officially christened as a paddle."

"So does that mean it's my turn to bend you?" he asked.

"You tell me. I have everything I want now, but you can see if I'm still wet." He slid a finger into my pussy, and I pushed myself onto his hand. He flipped me around and shoved me flat across the desktop, which was still warm from his ordeal. I felt his soft fingers spread my cheeks wide apart. I knew what was coming next. I looked back and saw his beautiful cock, bare and aiming straight for my target.

"Hey, fucking is fine, but no breeding in my barn!" I yelled back to him.

He quickly dug through his boss's drawers and found a condom. (Obviously the manager's office was not only used for office duties.) Once properly sheathed, he got back behind me and fucked me in true mindless animal style. I held on to the sides of the desk and raised my ass in the air to take as much as I could of him until finally I felt his cock pulse one last time inside my pussy. My own juices ran down my thighs and into my leather boots.

I called him the next day. He ended up with some light bruising on his buttcheeks from the paddle and I had hip bruises from being slam-fucked against the hard desk, but nobody was complaining. My new serving board now hangs proudly in the kitchen, awaiting the next hoedown at the breeding barn.

PINK CHEEKS

Fiona Locke

Ever been spanked?"

Charles's question catches me totally off guard. "What?"

"You heard me, Emma. Have you ever been spanked?"

I've been so focused on my computer screen it takes several seconds for me to register what he's asking. "What, you mean as a kid?"

My coworker grins slyly at me. "Well, that too," he drawls, waiting for me to catch on. His bright blue eyes sparkle with mischief, making me blush. "No, later. When you grew up. The adult kind."

The truth is that I haven't, though I've always secretly wanted to be. But there's no way I'm telling *him* that.

I don't believe it. He's trying to make me confess to having kinky fantasies, but I'm not going to admit it until *he* does. Besides, it's too much fun playing dumb. "What are you talking about? Only kids get smacked."

Charles laughs. "Silly girl. I'm talking about the sexy kind.

The *erotic* kind. You've got to know what I mean."

Jolted, I peer over the top of our cubicle for a quick glance around the office. "Will you keep your voice down?" I plead, my ears burning.

He rolls his chair closer to me, and I tilt my computer screen away from him. He lowers his voice to a conspiratorial whisper. "Erotic spanking," he repeats. "That's what I'm talking about. With a lover."

I stare at him blankly for a moment, then feign illumination. "Ohh," I say. "I get it! You mean…" I shake my head and look away, laughing. A lover, indeed. Everyone knows the roses I got on my birthday last month came from the receptionist.

But he won't let go of his line of questioning. "That's right," he says, his eyes invading me with their frankness. "So you haven't done it, but have you ever *thought* about it?"

This is too much. I'm going to die of embarrassment if he keeps this up. "Have *you*?" I retort.

Now he glances at his computer, and I suddenly wonder what he's working on. Is he even working at all? Or just surfing dirty websites? I lean back in my chair and crane my neck around to see, but he quickly turns the screen away.

"Uh-huh," I say triumphantly. "Just as I thought. You know they keep a record of every website we visit, don't you?"

Charles dismisses my warning with a wave of his hand, but I happen to know for a fact that one of the guys in Human Resources was sacked last year for exactly that. He'd been downloading split-crotch shots from some busty bimbo site, saving them to his hard drive here at work so his wife wouldn't find them. I can't imagine Charles looking at anything that unimaginative, but still…

My words have had an effect, though, and he appears to be closing down whatever page he was on. He glances over at me with a cryptic smile. "Doesn't hurt to be cautious," he says.

I turn back to my own screen and furtively finish reading the story he had interrupted. One of the author's best, a little tale about a Victorian gentleman and his naughty maid. Squirming, I type a quick, appreciative response and then shut down the newsgroup. Websites aren't safe, but I can download the newsgroup posts with my email. They don't read our private correspondence.

I sense Charles watching me out of the corner of his eye. His interrogation has got my dirty mind working overtime, and I can almost imagine I'm broadcasting my thoughts to him. Can he smell my arousal?

Shifting in my seat, I force myself to get back to work.

"You still here, then?"

I glance up at the voice. Grant, always the last one to leave, is putting on his coat. Charles is still at work beside me in the cubicle. I must have lost track of the time.

"Afraid so," I sigh. "Got to finish this report."

Charles waits a beat before nodding. "Yeah. Me, too."

"Well, I'm calling it a day," Grant says. "One of you will have to lock up." He hands the keys to Charles, even though I'm closer.

Charles bids him a pleasant evening and an odd look passes between the men as Charles pockets the keys. I listen to the sound of Grant's footsteps moving down the corridor and out the front door.

Now my coworker turns to me, the cryptic smile on his face. "We're alone," he states. An insinuation. A threat. A promise.

"So we are," I say, forcing a cool smile of my own. "Well, back to work."

"Oh, no." He rises slowly from his chair and comes to me, reaching across me for my mouse.

"What are you—?"

Before I can protest, he's navigated his way to a master directory revealing the source and destination of posts from a newsgroup with a very conspicuous name. I gasp.

"My, my," he says. "What a naughty girl."

I blush furiously and look away. This is surreal. It's like a story straight from the newsgroup. There's no doubt in my mind what's coming next. And there's no question that I'll submit.

Charles takes me by the hand, and I go meekly where I am led. I don't lift my head until we reach the break room, which smells of tepid brown water and stale pastries. He guides me directly to the single wooden straight-backed chair in the room. The very same chair I've talked about with my imaginary friends on the newsgroup. It's the one I always use, squirming on the hard seat as I fantasize about the pain of a spanking. At last the penny drops.

"*Victorian Schoolmaster*," I say in an awed whisper.

Charles gives me the evil grin he signs all his posts with. It's far more effective in person. "*Pink Cheeks*," he replies.

I giggle, hearing my moniker aloud for the first time.

"This is no laughing matter, young lady," he says sternly.

My reply is automatic. "No, sir." It's how I've addressed him in writing numerous times. But actually saying it to him…I'm trembling with fear, anticipation, ecstasy, and a thousand other things there are no emoticons to express.

"You know what you need."

I'm not sure if it's a question or a statement, but I know how I'm meant to respond in any case. "Yes, sir," I whisper.

"Good girl."

A palpable silence follows. Enough time for all to become clear. "Victorian Schoolmaster" began posting to the group a few weeks after I did. So he must have known all along. That was months ago. I quiver at the thought. How many hundreds of posts have I made in that time? How many fantasies have I described in explicit detail? Worst of all—how many of his stories have I gushed over, declaring them my favorite masturbation aids?

I look up to see Charles peering intently at me, reading my thoughts.

"Oh, yes, my dear," he says with deep satisfaction. "I know all about your kinky little mind. I know all your hot buttons and trigger words. And I intend to make full use of that knowledge." He pauses before adding, "You've earned yourself a sound spanking, young lady, and you're about to learn what a well-smacked bottom feels like. You naughty, naughty little girl."

The words nail me one by one. He's a fantasy come to life before my eyes. I'd even been tempted to write about him on the newsgroup—a fantasy about my handsome coworker with the vivid blue eyes—but something held me back. Now I'm immensely relieved about that.

With slow deliberation he indicates the chair and I chew my lip. I know what he wants and I know better than to pretend I don't. Obediently, I place the chair in the center of the room and return to stand in front of Charles, my head down.

"Now then, little miss," he says, eyeing me sternly, just like the Victorian schoolmaster he plays so well online. "I think you know what comes next."

I do. As if in a dream, he seats himself in the austere chair, his trousers taut over firm muscular thighs. I stare at his lap, dizzy.

I sink into position and place my clammy hands on the floor. I never thought I'd be seeing the ugly yellow lino this close.

Charles's hand rests on my bottom and I am still, as though frozen by a spell. He pats me gently over my tailored skirt and then slowly begins to raise it. I lift my hips to help him tug it up over my rear.

"Naughty little girls," Charles says, "who read naughty little stories deserve to have their naughty little bottoms smacked."

I shudder at the words, blood rushing loudly in my ears as my heart hammers in my chest.

He caresses my bottom and I writhe over his knees, imagining his approval as he sees the panties I've described on the newsgroup. The ones that make me feel like a schoolgirl again. Without a word, he slips his fingers into the waistband of my white cotton knickers, pulling them down to expose me. I flush with embarrassment, my face burning.

Now his palm rests on my bare skin. The stifling room drops twenty degrees as the erotic dread consumes me. Helpless, I shiver and lie trembling across his thighs. For a moment—just a moment—I want to leap up and run. Call it off, scurry away, and hide forever. But I know I won't. I *can't.*

"Discipline, Emma," my stern schoolmaster says, "is something you clearly need. And I intend to teach you a firm lesson. You've had this punishment coming for a long time."

"Yes, sir," I moan. It's all I'm capable of saying.

Then I feel his palm lift from me. I hold my breath. The hand seems to hang suspended in the air forever before coming down to meet my skin with a loud smack. Startled by the reality of the situation more than by the pain, I yelp. Another smack, another yelp. Another and another and another. I'm feverish with embarrassment and desire as he spanks me briskly, thoroughly, not neglecting a single inch of vulnerable flesh.

"Blatant disregard of the rules," he chides. "And what has it earned you, young lady? A good sound spanking." A particularly hard volley of smacks punctuates these words and I cry out even louder.

When he finally stops, I moan softly, writhing over his lap. *Don't stop,* I try to tell him with my body. But he does. The warm glow in my backside is comforting. It matches the one on my face. He urges me up and I struggle gracelessly to my feet, unable to look at him.

"I'm not finished with you, my girl," Charles says. He waits for me to look up at him before adding, "Your hairbrush. Go and collect it."

I blush even more fiercely, now truly mortified. Of course. He knows all about that, too. The antique ebony one I found on eBay and described to the group in loving detail. I carry it in my bag and every time I brush my hair with it, I imagine a no-nonsense authority figure using it on my backside.

My hands are shaky and sweaty as I hurry to obey, fumbling the hairbrush out of my handbag and nearly dropping it as I present it to him.

Charles smacks it against his hand, making me wince. "Back over my knees," he orders.

My legs have forsaken me. I collapse into position.

He lays the cool wood against my burning flesh, and I utter a little mouselike squeak. He smoothes it over every inch of reddened skin, making me squirm even more. I close my eyes and brace myself. I've never even had the courage to spank myself with it; I have no idea how it will feel.

Charles taps it against my bottom. "Prepare yourself, young lady. This will teach you a lesson you'll never forget."

The first stroke connects and I arch wildly on his lap, crying out at the pain. He doesn't give me time to recover before delivering the next one, and the next.

I'm astonished at the pain. I never imagined it would hurt this much. I'd read and written about countless hairbrush spankings, but never truly understood the sensation. It's terrible and wonderful at once, especially when I'm at the mercy of a skilled and uncompromising disciplinarian.

I breathe into each stroke, hissing through my teeth, yelping as the wood strikes my tender flesh. When I struggle, he holds me firmly in place. I'm helpless. Delirious. Flying.

After a dozen strokes, he finally stops. I lie gasping and panting over his lap. I see him set my hairbrush down on the table in front of me, and I melt with relief.

"Have you learned the value of discipline?" he asks.

"Yes, sir," I whimper.

"Good girl." He trails his fingertips over my punished bottom. Then he squeezes my burning cheeks, making me squeal.

He gives a soft laugh. Then he helps me up again. And sits there, silent. Waiting.

I can't play dumb and wouldn't dare try. He knows me inside out. He knows every single element in my fantasy life, and he relishes exploiting them. "Thank you for punishing me, sir," I say.

Charles smiles and rises to gather me in his arms, stroking me like a cherished pet. His hands stray to my tender bottom and he squeezes, making me yip.

"Pink Cheeks," he says fondly. "I think you'll be staying behind tomorrow night as well. And the night after that."

I bury my face in his chest, tingling all over with sensations I don't quite know how to process yet. My first spanking. I can hardly wait to write about it. I know my favorite imaginary friend will respond.

PAGE BY PAGE

Laura Bacchi

He called me Lilly at first. Well, all of my clients did, because that was the name I gave them, but it was the way he said it—slowly, exaggerating the Ls, that kind of thing. And he said it a lot, always referring to me in the third person. *Lilly will take off her skirt now. Lilly will remove her hose....*

It was creepy as hell at first but when you need the money, and the pain, you get used to it. You give the guys the whole fantasy. One day he put me in the stocks, then sat down and read to me for his full two hours. My first thought? If he wanted to waste his money on words, that was his problem. But I quickly figured out the words he spoke were his own...and that he was writing about me or, more specifically, he was writing about the things he wanted to do to me. Things he wasn't allowed to do. As a professional submissive, I had rules: No touching me directly. No sex. But in his stories—and he wrote a lot of them—he did it all. He'd come in me and on me. Invite his friends over without my permission. Tie me up and never let me go.

These tales—red flags, every one of them—didn't make me cancel our weekly appointments. I was too intrigued to ban him and too turned on to stop the string of loosely connected stories starring him, his toys, and my body. Then he changed the rules of the game by beginning each new story with "Lilly" only to switch to another female name later in the tale. He'd watch me as he made the change, waiting for any reaction on my part.

Today he got one. Today he tried the name Sarah.

My body tensed for a split second. He stopped speaking, shifted in his chair and smiled. He knew. I'd been careful, hiding my mail before a client came over, locking up all my personal stuff before *I* got locked up, but still he found out.

"Lucky guess?" I asked. He liked me to talk during our sessions, so I hoped he didn't mind my asking.

"I believe in making my own luck, Sarah."

I gulped at this second mention of my name. So he'd been poking around. Or maybe he'd talked to the right person or perhaps peeked in my mailbox that day it came late. I didn't really care how he'd found out. In a way, it was a relief, but him knowing my real name had me on edge. Had him blurring the line between a professional relationship and something personal.

I liked personal. I missed it like hell.

Our eyes met as he continued to read from the slim leather-bound journal in his hands, turning page after page as the minutes flew by. But he didn't look at the pages, and the words didn't come out choppy and hesitant like he was ad-libbing from that point on. No, he'd memorized each husky syllable falling from those full, perfect lips. My mentor had warned me about this moment—the moment a sub ceased to see a paying Dom as a customer. "Once he knows he's got you, he'll stop paying. You'll let him. And you'll forget about the limits."

I glanced at the clock radio on the table by his chair and the phone beside it. Soft music would fill the room at exactly 8:00 p.m. to let him know playtime was over. He'd release me from the stocks, ask me if I needed anything—a glass of water, a rub down, depending on our play—then he'd leave. If I didn't call in by 8:10, my safety net would call me.

"Are you listening to me, Sarah?"

Not really. I was too busy wondering what would happen if he got up while he read and unplugged the clock or took the phone off the hook.

"Yes, I'm listening." None of this *Sir* or *Master* shit for him. He didn't like it.

"I don't believe you, Sarah. What did I just read?"

You're not reading anything, I wanted to say. *You're making it up as you go, hoping I'll want this.* And I did want this. Today's story was…different. Simpler. Just me and him and his open palm against my ass. Plus he'd ditched the third person crap after figuring out my real name. My heart kicked against my ribs in double time. He was hitting close to home. Too close. I checked the clock again. We had an hour and a half to go.

"You said you were going to spank me."

His laugh was soft. "Close, Sarah. I said, 'I'm going to spank you with my hand until I turn your sweet ass pink. Then red. I'll spank until you cry for me to stop, then cry for me to never let it end.' Will you bruise for me, Sarah? Will you cry with just my hand?"

"You know that's not allowed."

"But you've cried for me before. You like to cry."

No one made me tear up and whimper like he did… A spasm ran deep through my cunt at the thought of how he could make me feel. "You know what I mean. Only your toys can touch me. No skin-to-skin contact at all." My reminder, reluctant to leave my lips, sounded small in the room. I felt small.

He left his chair and walked to where I stood bent at an awkward angle. He still held the book. The solid outline of his erection filled my view. I licked my lips and wished it would fill my mouth instead.

He leaned down to whisper in my ear. "I hadn't forgotten the rules."

No "Sarah" this time. Just hot breath in my ear, and, before he stood again, his lip grazed my earlobe. "But you want me to touch you."

I shook my head, but moisture gathered between my pussy lips to betray me should he bother to check. *Focus,* I told myself. *You're about to lose control.* So I focused on the long, thin journal, its faded brown cover with a chunk missing from the back corner, like a dog had bitten it. Or maybe it was the front. I wanted to see inside it, to see his handwriting. Would it be neat and tidy? Fluid and graceful? Or perhaps he printed in all capitals, each letter as precise as his aim on my flesh with his tails and paddles.

As he rose away from me, the book slid from his grasp. Maybe I wasn't the only one losing control. It landed spine down and open, the pages quickly flipping past to offer me a glimpse of…nothing. He hadn't written a fucking thing.

He picked up the diary.

"Why didn't you write in it?" I asked.

"Seems like a waste, doesn't it?"

I nodded as best I could in the stocks. "The stories, they're very good. Definitely publishable."

"But do you want to live them?"

"Some. A few you've shared aren't my style."

He circled around me. I pictured him behind me, gazing straight at my pussy to see if it was wet.

"You apparently liked today's."

"Yes. Sometimes all that black leather seems so cliché. Your hand—"

"Is that an invitation, Sarah?"

"The *idea* of your hand," I corrected myself. "That pleases me."

"Then let me please you."

He came back in front of me and set the journal on the stocks, right above my head, then braced his hands on either side of my captured ones below. Face-to-face, we bumped noses, and I inhaled his scent, stronger than usual for this early in our appointment. Perspiration covered his forehead. His nose barely touched mine, but I knew he was testing me. If he didn't stop it, I'd fail miserably and beg him to break all the rules.

"I do plan to use the book," he whispered. He must have given the book a nudge because it slid from its perch and fell onto my back. I jumped but the journal stayed flat against the space between my shoulder blades. "I plan to use it today. Unless you let me touch you."

I closed my eyes. He waited for my consent patiently as I grappled with the harm this one little slip would cause me. Would he tell another client? Did he know any other clients? If so, he was asking me to commit professional suicide. Even if he didn't know anyone or didn't talk, I would be opening myself up to a whole new set of rules. Or perhaps no rules at all.

I shifted my bare feet on the cold cement below. Checked the clock again and swallowed. My mouth had gone completely dry.

"No. I'm sorry."

He exhaled heavily, as if he'd been holding his breath while waiting for my answer. I felt his disappointment, felt it in my half-liquid bones and in the hesitant clenching of my pussy. Not hesitant enough, however—I was drenched and the soft, wet sound of my juices filled the air.

"Are you sure about that, Sarah?"

When I nodded, he walked to my side and lifted the journal from my spine. I went completely rigid when the faintest touch of something trailed down my ribs because I couldn't tell if it was his finger or a corner of the book. My mind took turns hoping it was one or the other. His breath tickled my hip.

"Where does one cross the line, Sarah? When our appointment is over, do you say good-bye, then make yourself come like I do?"

This one little confession wouldn't hurt…would it?

"Yes," I admitted.

"Then let me make you come. Let me touch you."

His warmth now hovered over the curve of my ass, and I trembled. I couldn't help it. The shiver rolling through my body forced me to make contact with the roughness of his five o'clock shadow and the smooth edge of two lips as they took a chance to make the connection linger.

"Who's touching whom?" he asked against me, the side of his lips wetting my asscheek.

I lowered my bottom half as best I could and he began messing with the book, the empty pages fluttering like whispered secrets against my skin. A corner of the journal glided over the entrance to my ass, then probed my slick hole below.

"Spread your legs."

I went wide, tilting my ass up for him. Giving him access. The book retreated for a heartbeat or two until he pressed the edge of one cover securely against the side of my clit. He tested me, pushing into my swollen flesh or pulling back, while I reacted, body tense, breath shallow. Then the blank pages flew past, blowing air over my soaked cunt as they returned to the swollen knot of my clit. I rolled my hips to control the pressure, to make the pages hit where I wanted them to.

"You're like an open book," he told me. "Do the others see it?" He fanned the book over my clit again. "Do they?"

"No."

No, they don't see anything. Not like you do. The others, they came in and did what they needed to do, then probably grabbed a quick lunch and got back to their corner offices. The night appointments went home to their wives and kids. In the end, I was just an outlet; they used me to get stuff out of their system, things they couldn't do with the wife or the girlfriend.

But with this guy, I was more than that. So when he removed the book and brought it flat against my right cheek, I was ready to do more than take it like I take the money. I was ready to feel. To enjoy.

He warmed me up nice and slow with the journal, each smack landing on a different part of my ass. Left. Right. The sides and dead center of each cheek. I savored the heat building on the surface, felt the burn reach my nipples as they dared to stretch farther toward the floor. He picked up the pace, let the book pound me harder now. Below the leather cover, my ass tingled and the flesh deeper inside each cheek opened up to the pain while I opened up, like a story. Page by page, each new word stripping back a layer here and there, pushing me—the real me—to unfold for him.

He dropped the book. I jumped at the noise it made—the thud of the leather and the flipping of pages. I knew what would happen next...his hand. His palm wide and hot against me. His fingers teasing the rosy splotches he'd made.

I waited. A fingertip trailed over the split of my ass. "It's just a toy," he whispered.

And I pretended to believe him. "I know," I said and spread my legs wider.

His other hand rested on the small of my back as the finger

continued to explore me. He found my cunt and slipped in to the last knuckle. After slowly pulling away, he smeared the wetness over my ass, then went back for more. I flooded into his fingers, three of them now, as he cupped them at my hole to gather all he could. After he'd painted me warm with my own juices, the spanking began again, each blow more relentless and perfect than the last. I was sweating, writhing in bliss, ready to come. But I wouldn't give him that pleasure. Not yet.

"I want to cry out your name. Your real name."

His smacks stopped. He gave it up reluctantly. "Paul," he told me, after several long seconds passed. So I came with that one syllable in my mouth and shouted it into the dank basement air over and over as he rubbed me to orgasm. My greedy slit pulsed with each spasm, wanting him there—cock or finger, hell, his whole fist—wanting anything to fill the void I felt there.

I went limp. He held me up, and my toes left the ground. I let them curl and uncurl at will. Let my wriggling body dance however it damn well pleased. I didn't expect him to start up again, but he did. He just kept smacking, no end in sight—a good thing, since I didn't want the beating to ever stop. He flicked his long fingers against my throbbing cheeks. The quick swipes stung like hell, better than any tails I'd tasted. He released my waist; I could barely stand, so he dragged over his favorite armchair and stuck it under my stomach. Then he stood between my dangling legs and let me have it—both hands, sometimes together, sometimes out of sync—until sobs wracked my chest.

"Easy, Sarah. We still have a while to go."

Did we? I couldn't see the clock through my tears. His fingers turned gentle, massaging the tender skin, giving me a chance to recover. He held my spent cunt gently, and I relaxed against his touch, never expecting the next smack to hit me there. When it did, I came beneath the smart little pops against my clit. And I screamed. Screamed and cried so fucking loud I didn't hear the music announcing the end of our session.

"Time's up." He was kissing my ass, no fingers on me at all. Only his lips.

He didn't unlock me. I could see the time now. Three minutes and I'd get a call. But I didn't want one. He must've been watching the clock too, because he unlocked me and carried me over to the phone with one minute left. My fingers fumbled to switch off the radio.

I dialed the number, unsure of what to say. My throat would be scratchy from my screams, plus it would be hard to say the words, "I'm all right." I wasn't all right. He shifted me in his lap until his fingers worked their way under my ass to lean me forward. The tips traced over the marks he'd made.

I'm not certain what I said to Marcie. She could probably tell something was up by the shakiness of my voice, but she didn't push it. I hung up. He took me down to the floor. The cool floor felt like heaven against my warm ass.

"Ever been spanked while being fucked?" he asked.

Of course I had. But not by him. Not by a paying customer. I didn't answer. I simply rolled over and got on all fours to offer him whatever hole he wanted.

"Tell me a story," I whispered against the uneven cement. "Tell me the story of Paul and Sarah."

Because I wanted to know where he saw this tale going. He'd pushed me out of my safety zone, and I'd gone down that road before. This time I wanted a happy ending, and when he spoke his next words, I knew he understood that I needed to keep some kind of distance. Just a little. Page by page he gave us a new story...

Sarah will spread her ass wide for me.
Sarah will take every inch.

FISCAL
DISCIPLINE

Simon Sheppard

There it was again, that ad on the Men Seeking Men board of Craigslist:

> Hot boy, 23, wants a gay guy to witness his punishment at the vicious hands of his female boss. No touching unless the boss demands it. Older perverts who enjoy seeing str8 boys in pain are especially welcome.

Hey, that was *me!*

Okay, as those of us who are into cheap, easy sex know, online cruising may be cheap, but it's rarely easy. It took literally days of emailed backing-and-forthing before the date was set up. And that was after I sent an only slightly Photoshopped photo of my face, the boy sent his body pic but not his face, and the woman involved refused to show me her face and made me swear discretion. Oh well, nobody ever said that being a slavering old sadist was gonna be easy.

The apartment was in one of those fancy new high-rises down-town, with minimalist furnishings and a view that must have been worth an additional five hundred a month. I'd been buzzed in by the doorman, taken the elevator while my dick swelled in anticipation, and been met at the apartment door by a skinny, naked young guy. Actually, the picture he'd sent hadn't shown how skinny he really was, how many tattoos he had, or how long—even soft—his uncut dick was. That was all, if not conven-tionally "hot," at least a pleasant surprise. And if his face had the hard-but-lost look of a street hustler...well, that was fine with me, too.

The biggest surprise, though, was Boss Lady, who was sitting in a Barcelona chair in the middle of the big white-on-white living room. It wasn't the ghastly flowered housedress she wore—the big shock was her face. Or rather, who she was. I mostly watch HBO and Showtime these days, but when I flip over to the financial news to see how my admittedly pathetic portfolio is doing, hers, more often than not, is the face I see: an anchor in one of the nation's major—and, reportedly, right-wing—media outlets. No wonder she wanted me to be discreet. But who, if push came to spanking, would take my word against hers? And anyway, this wasn't Pigeon Forge, Tennessee; in a city full of secular libertines, would anyone even care?

She sat there, one hand inside her loose dress, stroking her tit. "Hello, sir," she said to me in her familiar voice. And to the boy: "I told you that there would be trouble when the chief returned from Zurich." Zurich was a sweet touch.

Personal Assistant looked genuinely concerned and a little scared. Punishment scenes—and I've been part of a bunch of them—often seem a bit dubious to me. Assuming the scene is consensual, that means the bottom wants to be worked over. (Unless he's getting paid, which might, I realized, have been the case here.) In reality, the willing masochist is being rewarded for some transgression, real or imagined, right? If Masochist Assistant Boy really had been bad, wouldn't the sensible thing be to withhold the spanking? So this visible fear, whether real or feigned, added a piquant jolt to the scene. My dick, already stiff, gave a little throb or two.

My useless musings were interrupted by Boss Lady's voice, a command disguised as a question. "Would you like to sit over there, sir?" She gestured behind me, to another Barcelona chair. This was obviously a designer-furnished dungeon. As I sat down, I suppressed an urge to check for Mies's signature on the frame, but that was hardly what the afternoon was about. I'd just have to assume the chairs were the genuine article, not cheap knock-offs like mine. I slid down onto the leather seat.

"Come over here, you bad boy. Your carelessness has managed to lose the firm hundreds of thousands of dollars, asshole. Now you're going to get it," Boss Lady said, her voice sliding down a half octave, *"while the CEO watches."*

Boy padded over reluctantly, his extensive dick, now at half-mast, bobbing and weaving ahead of him. His body was mostly smooth, but his thin legs and butt were covered with thick black hair. Nice!

"Get across my fucking lap."

Assistant Boy didn't move. I looked at his thin, tattooed body and wanted to go over there, grab him, drag him over to my Barcelona chair, and administer a little administrative discipline myself, but that wasn't what had been arranged, and, call me old-fashioned, but when it comes to sadomasochism, I like to play by the rules. Still, I couldn't help but notice how his formerly soft cock was rapidly filling up with blood. Listen, I don't know about you, but to me, there are few sights more lovely than a skinny guy's big dick hoisting its way to full erection. You can keep your Sistine Chapel.

Boss Lady, though, seemed supremely unmoved by her assistant's burgeoning hard-on. I often wonder that about straight women: why they seem so less appreciative of dick than gay men are. It may be churlishly stupid to criticize that, though, since that just means more putatively straight prick for us queer cocksuckers to service. Whatever. The fact remained that Boss Lady was scowling at her underling in a way that could shake the stock market to its core. And that I desperately wanted to get out my dick and start wanking.

So I did, cautiously unzipping my fly, reluctant to incur the wrath of Boss Lady. She clocked my whipping it out, but said nothing, just solemnly nodded. Then she turned to her reluctant assistant once again. "I told you to get your fucking ass over here, you fucking shit." Her conservative employers would have been appalled. Or maybe not. You know what they say about those Republicans...

"Last warning," Boss Lady snarled, "before I call Security. And you can imagine how *they'll* handle this."

With a resigned expression and a stiff dick, the hapless assistant padded over to his doom. Now that his cock was pointed upward, I noticed how very big his balls, swinging as he walked, were. I gave my own shaft an extra little squeeze.

He stood before his irate employer, trembling slightly.

Boss Lady's hand was still inside her housedress, stroking. "Assume the position, asshole," she said.

"Yes, ma'am," the boy said meekly, resigned by now to his prearranged fate. He maneuvered himself down till he was straddling her lap, his furry ass pointed in my direction, his big balls visible, pressed against Boss Lady's flowered-chintz leg.

"You know why I'm doing this?"

"Not really, ma'am." He sounded genuinely afraid.

"Well, I suppose you deserve an education." She withdrew her hand from her robe, brought it up above the skinny boy's hairy ass, then brought it down with a resounding smack. "The kind you didn't get at Stanford."

Which is when her cell phone chimed. She looked over to the table where three phones were laid out side to side.

"That may be important. Bring the phone to me."

Executive Assistant Boy slid off his boss's lap and went over to the table to fetch the phone. There was a single pink handprint visible through the dark hair on his ass, and it was beautiful. He handed Boss Lady the Nokia, and when she answered it, her voice changed. She was no longer the nasty bitch-boss with a tenderized boy squirming on her lap, but a charming, slightly subservient career woman, albeit one whose non-phone hand was between her thighs, stroking away.

"Yes, sure I can do that," she said, sounding increasingly apologetic and, well, meek. "No, sorry. Yes, tell him by this evening at the latest."

She glanced over at me to see what my reaction to all this was. I, dick still in hand, was trying to give nothing away. I certainly wasn't going to slip and say something inane and scene-breaking—for instance, "Is that the network calling?" Not while there was the prospect of seeing a naked, hairy, skinny young man get what was coming to him. Finally, after what seemed like forever but was probably a minute or two at most, Financial News Anchorwoman hung up the phone and became Nasty Boss Lady once more.

"You think you're going to get away that easy?" she growled to her assistant. "Come over here and get on your knees." She spread her legs, pulled aside her housedress, and gestured to her shaved cunt. "And take care of this."

I have nothing against naked women, but when it comes to

pussy, I'm impassive. The sight of that subservient, skinny guy, his soon-to-be-abused butt toward me, going down on Boss Lady was, regardless, sweet. I stroked myself softly, lest I come too soon and bring my part of the proceedings to a premature close.

The misbehaving boy was apparently good at giving head: Boss Lady was soon panting with pleasure. But just when I thought the scene might be turning into something more vanilla, she pushed aside the boy's face.

"Back on my lap," she barked. "Now."

She rearranged him till I was getting the same good view as before. Then she stroked his furry ass and raised her hand.

"*This* will teach you to talk trash about hedge funds," she said grimly. And she brought her hand down firmly on the young man's left cheek. It was a hard slap, but not too hard, and I was none too sure whether Assistant squirmed in pleasure or in pain—or in a delightful combination of the two.

"And *this* will teach you to talk to investigative reporters," she said, and her hand came down, considerably harder, on the right side of his ass. No gentle ramping-up here.

"I'm so sorry, ma'am," the assistant said. "It won't happen again."

"Too late," she said, and this time her hand came down stingingly on the hairy crack of his ass. Assuming that the bottomboy had any nerves at all, that one must have hurt.

I had a sudden, giddy thought about "the invisible hand of the marketplace," and had to stifle a giggle. In any case, Boss Lady's hand was anything but invisible. She was as merciless as the global economy.

Her hand swung down on the errant errand boy's ass again and again, bringing a flush that soon morphed from meaty pink to a satisfyingly bright red. If it weren't for the copious hair on the bottomboy's butt, I'm sure I would have seen traces of broken capillaries. I figured that the only thing that could make the scene hotter would be to see the boy's presumably agonized face. So— not sure what the rules were, but knowing that if I really were a CEO, I would be able to do anything I fucking pleased—I stood up, cock in hand, and approached the spanking.

As the domme in the actual scene, Boss Lady would have been within her rights to object. As my employee within the role-play, she would defer to me, her superior. But as it happened, my famous hostess did neither, just looking up at me as I approached, then continuing to wale away on her hapless assistant's ass. She did keep up a steady flow of angry, accusative chatter, though. It was filled with investment terms I'd heard her use on the air— spiders, stock derivatives, and the like—but even at the best of times, I had only the vaguest idea of what most of them meant. Now, with my brain engorged by lust, she might as well have been speaking in tongues.

It was, yes, exciting to get close, so near to the action that I could damn near feel the heat radiating from the bottom's tortured ass. "Look at me," I said angrily, deciding to play the part of the demanding CEO. The unhappy executive assistant raised his head, and genuine tears were streaking his cheeks. It was almost more than sadistic old me could bear; I had to take my hand away to stop myself from coming.

"You see how angry you've made my chief?" Boss Lady growled, letting loose a rain of blows on the boy's already aching ass. "You'd better make it up to him."

The boy spoke through gritted teeth. I was sure I could see his eyes brimming with real tears. "How, ma'am? How can I do that?"

Boss Lady stopped slapping, her hand—which must have been aching itself by now—poised above the boy's bright red, furry butt. "You can suck his cock."

Now *that* was more like it.

"But...but...I've never..."

Whap! The sound echoed around the expensive walls.

"Do it, cuntboy. Now."

He raised his head to me. Yes, tears were running down his cheeks. He opened his mouth. I inserted my dick.

For someone who theoretically had never sucked cock before, the boy did a surprisingly excellent job. Even when Boss Lady resumed her spanking, I didn't feel his teeth, not much.

I did, however, feel a powerful urge to spew sperm. And I had a suspicion that bottomboy was getting perilously close to his limits, which was confirmed when Boss Lady looked up at me, nodded, and mouthed the single word, "Come."

So I did, pulling out of the young man's mouth at the last minute and spraying his face with jism, my liquid protein mixing with his tears.

Well, I'm one of those fellows who comes enthusiastically, then loses interest rapidly. So when Boss Lady said, "I think that's enough punishment for you. For now," I felt something approaching relief. My part in the little tableau having apparently come to a damp end, I wiped my dick off, licked the sperm from my hand, and zipped up. I was done.

"You can show the CEO out now," said Boss Lady in a commanding voice.

Her underling, his face still wet with two kinds of salt, struggled up from his domme's lap. The fellow's cock was still, fairly amazingly, hard as a rock, and there was a wet spot on the chintz housedress. I hoped he hadn't leaked precome on the pricey leather of the Barcelona chair.

"Thank you very much for coming, sir," he said as he showed me to the door. The lock clicked behind me. I found myself idly wondering what would happen between the two of them now.

More spanking? A cuddle and a kiss? The exchange of cash? Whatever. The moment had, in its way, been quite perfect. As I headed down the sidewalk, en route to my considerably less deluxe apartment, I mused on power, playacting, and the close of trading on the Big Board.

And when, a few weeks later, the head of a major energy firm got busted for sucking dick in a public restroom, I found it delightful to watch Boss Lady on the air, solemnly pontificating on the lamentable decline of morality in American public life. Hell, I had to stifle a giggle.

Late capitalism. You gotta love it.

PRE-PARTY

Thomas S. Roche

It's just a little meet and greet before the event; you know, get relaxed, get acquainted, get a cab—nothing big.

Their guests are already dressed when they arrive, but of course, as always, Jessa's the last one to suit up. She's spent the whole day slicing crudités and assembling complicated hors d'oeuvres and other comestibles she's studied in the pages of esoteric European magazines, which is essentially what she rushes into the bedroom to do when everyone starts to show up. The main exception is that in this case, the comestible to be assembled is her.

Justin's left on the couch in his tight leather pants, high boots and wifebeater, making kinky conversation with Tara from the kinky head shop and her girlfriend (or girl friend? He's not sure) named Raven or Blackbird or something, Sherry from the local leather group and her boyfriend what's-his-name (whom Justin isn't entirely sure he likes), Mike from the gay bar and his new boyfriend from Denmark or Holland or Sweden or something,

Jens or Jurgen or Jan. They're all strapped to the nines, Mike in the leatherboy uniform; Sven in slick rubber; Tara in a PVC WAC uniform; Sherry in a corset and miniskirt; Boyfriend, kinda lamely, in a black leather duster; short-haired, butch-of-center Raven in PVC pants and halter and thigh-high boots—she's got an overcoat in the hall closet. They're all sipping cocktails and nibbling canapés; nibbling, for most of them, because with clothes this tight there's not really anywhere for most of it to go.

The cocktails, however, they manage to find room for plenty of. For the first ten minutes of Jessa's "quick" shower—she's notorious—Justin freshens the cocktails, but pretty soon the bottles have found their way over and everyone's freshening his own; the conversation gets raunchier and before too much longer Sherry's been dragged over Mike and Sven's laps and the two of them are trading off giving her hard spanks while she giggles and then softly begins to moan.

This seems kind of weird to Justin—like the things you hear are supposed to happen at San Francisco parties before fetish balls, but never do. Well, it's happening, and Sherry's odd boyfriend doesn't seem to have a strong opinion one way or another, but from the slowly rising moans and softly dwindling giggles, Sherry certainly does. Justin shifts uncomfortably; Mike has pulled up Sherry's tight latex skirt and from where he's sitting, Justin can see quite clearly that she is not wearing much at all underneath.

In fact, as the spanking continues, Mike takes an entirely uncalled-for liberty, playfully plucking the crotch of Sherry's G-string out of the way, giving Justin a crotch shot that reveals smooth lips flushed with excitement. Boyfriend gets a funky look on his face, staring daggers or giving a mental high-five, Justin isn't sure. What he *is* sure about is that he has to shift quite nervously and attempt a little hippy-shake to pop his cock out of its awkward down-pointing position, because it's getting harder by the moment, no less when Mike invites him to fondle Sherry a little.

"Oh, I don't think so," says Justin meekly. "But thanks." *How do gay guys get away with this?* he's thinking, but he already knows the answer, or perhaps knows that there is no meaningful answer, and besides, he's less concerned about the sociopolitical ramifications of Sherry getting fingered than he is about whether his cock is going to snap in half if he doesn't shuffle it.

"Finger her butt!" guffaws Boyfriend bizarrely, out of the blue, and Justin makes his decision: he doesn't like the guy. What a freak.

"That is a naughty boyfriend you've got," says Jens, the exchange vaguely comical in his Dutch/Danish/Icelandic accent, and Justin manages to sneak a hand along his crotch to readjust the damn thing, but he gets it all wrong and now his cock's jammed into the waistband of his leather pants. He softly says "Motherfuck," asking himself for the dozenth time why he's self-conscious about adjusting his dong when a girl he only vaguely knows is being fingered a few feet away and oh, incidentally, the lesbians are going at it pretty hot and heavy, making out, with Raven's hand between Tara's thighs, pretty far up under the hem of that WAC skirt. Things are getting interesting, but all Justin can feel is awkward. Even though he's wearing leather-butch drag, he's not much of a public top, even in his own home. Besides, he and Jessa didn't have that conversation yet—there were too many hors d'oeuvres to make. Limits? Boundaries? Who the fuck knows?

"Hey, baby?" comes Jessa's voice from the top of the stairs. Justin has never been so relieved in all his life; it gives him the perfect excuse to get up and leave the scene. His relief only lasts a moment, though, because as he walks his mostly-hard dick goes wrenching down into the elastic of his boxer-briefs' left leg, and he's right back in discomfort-ville.

"Need something?" he calls up the stairs, his voice as pleasant as he can make it—and fairly pleasant, really, all things considered.

"I need help getting into my dress. Can you send one of the girls up?"

Justin shoots a look at the couch area; Tara and Blackbird are definitely in dishabille; Sherry is most definitely occupied as Boyfriend periodically yelps, "Spank her!" and "Smack 'er butt!"

Justin races up the stairs, pausing halfway to stick his hands down his leather pants and adjust his cock; he breathes a sigh of relief. He runs the rest of the way up to the bedroom door and opens it. Jessa is stark naked; she whirls, gasps, covers herself with her hands, tits only, freshly-shaved pussy still visible. Justin's eyes go wide, then he gives her a wicked smile.

"I *said* send one of the girls!"

"They're all busy," says Justin, eyeing Jessa up and down lasciviously. "All of a sudden you're afraid to let me see you naked?"

She glances at the bed, where an immaculate black rubber minidress with a tomato red stripe down the side sits alongside a pair of rubber panties and a bottle of cornstarch baby powder.

"I didn't want you to see my dress until I'm ready," she says with a flirty smile. "It's a surprise."

"I'm surprised," smiles Justin, and moves closer to Jessa. For an instant it seems like she's going to move away, but then she melts into him and as his arms go around her he feels the smoothness of her well-dried flesh; four damp towels form a trail from the bathroom, terminating in a limp pair of thigh-high black latex boots, a stripe on the outside of each the exact tomato red of the stripe on the dress.

"Amazing," he whispers.

She feels the bulge in his leathers just as his finger finds she's not dry all over. She wriggles deeper onto him and he fingers her until she whimpers, then pushes him away.

"Everybody's waiting," she says. "I need to get dressed."

"They've got crudités," says Justin. "And drinks." He smiles evilly. "And I'm sure they can entertain themselves."

She comes close, kisses him, rubs his cock through his pants. "You can fuck me at the party," she whispers. "They've got that great back alley behind the standing cage." She pulls away; he gropes after her, but she dances out of reach. "Help me get my dress on?"

"If you insist," he says, eyeing her naked body.

"I have to put the boots on first," she says, sitting on the edge of the very high four-poster bed. His thoughts go evil places: How many times has he had her tied to that bed? How desperately does he want to tie her to it *right now?* She lifts one sockless foot into the air as she pulls on one high boot. *She's not going to be able to walk much without socks*, thinks Justin; then again, he's not sure he wants her to.

Jessa wiggles her foot at him. "Zip?"

Justin gets close enough to smell her, his fingers caressing the zipper as he draws it over her ankle, up her calf, past her scrumptious knee, and up the inside of her thigh. His hand keeps moving. Two fingers go into her, easy as pie, before she can close her legs. She slips back onto the bed, arches her back, moans.

"Stop," she gasps, wriggling her way off of him. She's smiling, but flushed, breathing hard. She kicks him away playfully with her high-heeled latex domme boot; she squirms her shapely foot into the other boot, then shoots him a wicked look, knowing what's coming. With this one, he takes his time zipping, letting his hands travel more slowly, and she lets him fuck her a little, two fingers inside her and a thumb on her clit, her legs spread, her body looking magnificent, naked except for those boots. He goes to lunge onto her. She pulls and rolls away, seizing the cornstarch.

"Powder me," she orders, handing him the bottle and putting up her arms. He frowns, scowls, dusts cornstarch onto his palms and begins rubbing them all over her. He starts with her breasts, because how can he not? She moans softly as his dusted palms work her nipples. He rubs down lower, turns her around, does her back, dusts her ass, spends more time on her breasts, her nipples now even harder, more sensitive, more responsive to the gentle pinches he gives her.

"You were going to let Sherry do this?"

"Maybe," she sighs softly. "With a few minor variations."

Bending over so that her naked, cornstarch-dusted ass rubs against the swell of his leather-clad cock, she reaches out and gets the dress. She stands, and he takes it from her, stretches it, holds it for her to slide her arms into, then pulls it over her head and gently pulls it down over her body: shoulders, breasts—going very slowly, caressing as he does—belly, ditto—then hips, and as he snugs the dress down over her thighs to the point where it's just barely decent, she wriggles to help him settle it, and he decides the last thing he wants is this fucking dress *settled.*

She doesn't even realize what's happening; he's bent her over the edge of the bed and has one hand on his belt, the other circling her wrist. She gasps, squirms a little, struggles, pushes back, starts to fight, weakly. When he kicks her booted feet apart, she does not pull them back together; she does not wriggle out of his grasp, and when the zipper goes down and his cock comes free, her hand gropes after it—but no, that's not how she's going to have him. He grabs her free wrist and pins it with the other up high in the small of her back, bending her over harder, shoving her against the bed as he surges onto her. She's played the tease, now she'll play the victim.

He holds her wrists tight and pins her to the bed. He wants to enter her without preliminary, taking her violently, savagely—but he stops at the last minute, holding his pinned captive and biting the back of her neck so hard she surges and writhes against him, crying out. His cockhead teases and rubs her lips, smooth with razor and lotion and cornstarch, in that order, slick with pussy juice and precome, in *that* order. Then as he pins her wrists behind her, holding them tighter than ever, he uses his other hand to open up the swollen lips of her sex and his cockhead finds her center.

He's in her with a single smooth thrust, and she tries to stifle it, the scream, but she can't. With the second thrust, deep into her, it's midway between a cry and a yelp; then it's all moan, slow and soft, as he begins to fuck her rapidly, not giving her a chance to acclimate, just taking her, using her, giving her stroke after stroke and not caring that he's going to come well before she can.

But then he remembers their wicked plan for the evening—a surreptitious, forbidden fuck, in that dark corner behind the standing cage, and Jessa climaxing desperately on his cock because, ever the Boy Scout, he's thought ahead.

He no longer needs both hands; the one pinning her wrists is a nice touch, but his cock's doing a fine job of holding her lips open wide as he slides in and out of her. He reaches into his tight leather pants, the belt buckle rattling and making her gasp a little as its coldness grazes her skin. He comes out with a tiny push-button vibrator, the size of a robin's egg.

She never sees it coming. He's into her all the way again, so deep that when he pushes the vibe up against her clit he can feel her muscles contracting around his cock. But she holds him too tight; he wants her too bad. As he fucks wildly into her, he realizes they're not going to hit it together. Holding the vibrator in place, he stops, all the way inside her; he breathes hard, he shudders, he freezes. Every muscle in his body goes tense. He pulls out and his head swells her entrance. She arches her back and shoves herself back onto him.

Fuck it, he figures, and starts thrusting smoothly into her; it takes maybe three strokes before it happens. He lets out a long, savage groan. He heaves his body onto her and his hips piston as he pins her against the bed. She shoves back against his pressure, and he floods her with his come.

Jessa lets out a low sigh of satisfaction, obviously thinking she's finished, but nothing could be further from the truth. When he pulls out of her easily, a thick string of his come glistens between his cock and her sex. She goes to get up from under him, but he still pins her wrists. She seems puzzled for a moment.

"What about the guests?"

"By now I think Mike's probably bisexual," I said, "and I wouldn't be surprised if Sherry's boyfriend's gone gay."

She looks at him over her shoulder, her makeup a little messy, one eye open wider than the other.

"Huh?"

Without answering, he clicks off the vibe, holds her wrists tighter, leans over her, grabs the rubber panties, not caring a bit that they're both dribbling his come onto the floor. He has to let go of her wrists to do it, which is a disappointment since that's his biggest turn-on, pinning her wrists while he fucks her; he also has to nudge her legs closed, which is a disappointment since that's his second biggest turn-on. But it's all worth it, as he guides first one booted foot, then the other, up and through the legs of the rubber panties.

"What are you doing?" she whines meekly. "We've got to get to the party."

The cornstarch on her thighs is lost to sweat and friction, so the stroke of the rubber up her legs is not quite smooth, but it's worth it when he snuggles the formfitting panties over her sex, then tucks the vibe into it and squeezes.

"Oh, Jesus fucking Christ," she says, and a few other things, considerably louder, as he climbs onto the bed and drags her body over his lap, smearing the remnants of his come over her latex dress and not caring, pinning her wrists with his left hand while with his right he does something he knows she's wanted since the first time he playfully smacked her ass in the kitchen, around three, when she protested weakly that she had crudités to slice.

He pulls up her skirt and exposes her ass for a spanking.

"The guests," she says, her voice all bleating desperation as he rubs the crotch of the rubber panties, forcing the vibe against her clit so that she gasps. Then he draws back and his cupped hand comes down hard on one firm cheek of her ass. She utters a yelp, grinds her hips against him. The vibe visibly jiggles around; even in the tight rubber panties, it can't stay absolutely still. He brings his hand down again, feeling the taut clench and the give of her asscheek. This time she doesn't yelp; she moans.

He adjusts the vibe and lifts his hand. This blow makes her whimper, softly, as she fucks herself slowly and rhythmically against his lap, rubbing the vibe between her clit and his thigh while she presents herself, ass high, for his next blow.

He gives it to her, right on the sweet spot, knowing from experience that the burst of sensation is going right into her clit, or her cunt, or her asshole, or something, some magic part of her that's going to get her off, especially with the vibe buzzing crazily.

He starts spanking her faster, a blow every other second, one cheek to the other, then both, then her pussy, careful not to smack the vibe—that would hurt, and worse yet, it might break the damn thing. She's moaning and bucking, and he's let go of her wrists because she needs them to claw at the bed. His hand's in her mouth now; she's biting his palm, hard, as he spanks her rapidly, adjusting the vibe every dozen strokes or so to make sure it's right where it's supposed to be—on her clit, making her come.

But it's the spanking that pushes her over the edge, when he blows off the vibe and just lets it bounce and jiggle in there, and smacks her hard on one sweet spot and then the other, over and over again, faster, while she bites his palm until he's afraid she'll draw blood and is surprised he doesn't care—then she moans so loud he knows the guests downstairs are hearing it, and since he's sure they don't care, he doesn't care, but he probably wouldn't anyway.

She writhes until her face is pointing up a little and her back is straight, leaving her rigid across his lap; her eyes go wide, and he catches them—open, lost, empty, focused on nothing but the explosion of pleasure that's about to go through her. Then it happens, and her eyes go tightly shut, and she melts into him again, dissolving into the rapid blows of his open hand on her ass, bucking and humping and shuddering all over as she comes.

When she finally goes slack, she desperately gropes after the vibe to turn it off, but can't manage it, her hands are shaking so bad. He slips his hands into her rubber panties and turns off the tiny machine. Good thing the vibrator's waterproof. Inside, the panties are molten, juices leaking out onto his leather pants and dribbling onto the bed.

She takes a deep breath, goes sliding out of his lap, and lands on the floor with her head on his thigh.

"The guests," says Jessa. "We should get downstairs. How rude of us."

Justin smiles, caressing her face as another little set of spasms goes through her body.

"I'm pretty sure they're entertaining each other," he says. "But yes. We should get downstairs."

He helps her up, dries her off a little, and even adds some cornstarch. The vibe goes back in his pocket, and he doesn't even bother to rinse it off first. They've got a fetish ball to get to.

STILL LIFE WITH INFIDELS #56

M. David Hornbuckle

It's after midnight in the corroded, industrial area of Birmingham known as Ensley, the old steel town. A van is parked in the gravel drive in front of an aluminum-walled warehouse, one of dozens of mini–steel mills and foundries on this stretch of road, many of them abandoned. There's no amber glow from the vents near the roof to indicate that this facility is still being used. In days gone by, an old black man probably sat in there melting down scrap metal and forging it into small hardware accessories like the eyehooks Rob installed at the head and foot of his fold-out back-seat. On her stomach, blindfolded with a red velvet scarf, Amy's now secured to those eyehooks by her wrists and ankles.

Earlier, because the streets in Birmingham have a lot of hills and curves, Rob wondered if she'd be safe enough back there, so he drove slowly and carefully, trying to take flatter roads when possible. When he picked her up, Amy had been naked in bed. He'd let himself in with the key she gave him, made her put on a kimono and the blindfold, and then tied her hands with nylon rope before leading her slowly to the van parked outside. That much of the plan had been at her request. The rest was up to him.

He isn't quite sure what to do with her now. There's a sliver of moon, providing almost all the light, other than the faint glow of the dashboard panel and the green lantern of Vulcan in the distance. The streetlamps around here are all busted. Rob sits up front in the driver's seat with the armrest up and his feet planted in the aisle between the captain's chairs. Elbow on knee, chin on fist, he's been sitting there for several minutes, looking at her, waiting for inspiration to strike. Amy is facing the back windows, the knot of the blindfold blending among her red curls. Her pink and blue kimono twinkles with the occasional reflection of a star. She's short enough to lie almost flat on the folded-out seat, her hands at her head, tied to the eyehooks. Her feet are spread about a foot and a half apart, each tied to an eyehook at the other end.

Later, Rob will step down out of his captain's chair and slam the door shut, and he'll imagine what must be going through Amy's mind, wondering where he's going, how long he'll be away, what he's doing. He'll decide to take his time walking around to the side door, letting each crunchy step in the gravel ring out in the empty night. He'll look into the side windows to check if he can see anything. Because of the curtains and the darkness, he won't be able to see much unless he puts his face right up against the glass. Then he'll just make out her curved form, but the ropes won't be visible from the outside. The headlights of a car will pass, but he'll feel safe enough with the van blocking any view of him from the road. The van itself won't seem suspicious; these minimills work all night when they work at all because it's not economical to let the furnaces cool down.

A couple of days ago, when Amy brought up the kidnapping idea, they'd been lying on her bed in the late afternoon after making love, brainstorming about sexual adventures they might have together in the near future. She didn't want to know when it was going to happen. She'd be ready. That afternoon was the first time they'd seen each other in a few weeks. They are each at least partly to blame for the breakup of the other's marriage, and while they both wait for the divorces to be final, they've tried to give each other some space. She's living with some friends who had a spare room. He's living mainly in the van, showering at the gym. Now that they're reunited, he'll probably start crashing with her most nights.

Rob considers putting on some music, something ambient and bass-heavy that will echo in the rusty, industrial surroundings. These minimills in the shadows remind Rob of his father, who used to work in the steel mills, the big ones, with the monstrous smokestacks that form jagged dragon teeth north of town. His father got laid off in the '80s when the whole industry went to shit. After that, he worked a few odd jobs until Rob finished high school, and then the folks moved to Pennsylvania where there were still some jobs to be had for steel men. Rob stayed behind, went to college, got married, played guitar in bands, learned about computers. He's still figuring out what he wants to do.

Later, when Rob finally slides the door open and steps in, Amy will turn her head in his direction, the only movement she can make. He will pull up the back of her kimono, revealing one pale buttock and then the other. Lifting his hand, he'll flick his wrist and inflict a quick hard smack, not with the palm, but with his fingers. A good cracking sound, he knows, is all about the suppleness of the wrist and fingertips. She'll moan in response. He'll bend down and hover his lips there, a hair's length over the point of impact, so she can feel his cool breath there. Then he'll rear back and strike again. He'll spank her a few more times, relishing the echo of each collision of his fingertips with her ass. Each blow will be accompanied by a squeal, a groan, or a "Yes." He'll hold his hand there, about an inch over her cheek, and he'll be able to feel the heat it emanates. Even in the relative dark, he'll see that she's turning as red and hot as molten steel. Again, he'll blow on it softly to cool it down. When that one cheek has nearly had enough, the other will still be white, unrefined, raw, ripe for smelting. He'll draw back his hand then and begin working that side, taking moments between each smack to check the color, temperature, and softness. From time to time, he'll spank the first cheek again to keep it fresh and supple. Soon Amy will begin to squirm, but the sounds she makes will reveal only pleasure.

That afternoon when they last saw each other before tonight, Amy had called him. Her soon to be ex-husband had been by to tell her that he wanted back some of the things she'd taken, some wedding presents. He'd said that certain friends specifically wanted him to keep those gifts. He'd actually used the word "adulterer," and Amy had said that it sounded so strange and archaic. It sounds that way to Rob also. On the phone, they admitted they missed each other, and Amy said it had been enough time. They'd made their point. Besides, she really needed comforting, and Rob is one of the only people she knows she can still count on after all they've done.

Summer stars gaze down from overhead, and the summer triangle of Vega, Deneb, and Altair is most bright. The sky is filled with animals—the swan, the bear, the eagle. There is also Perseus, and of course Rob's star sign, Scorpio. In the bushes there are animals also, a set of small yellow eyes, probably a possum or a raccoon. There are thin patches of woods all along this road, between the warehouses and foundries, with as many empty beer bottles as trees. These patches of woods are almost more like weeds or parasites, encroaching on industry, rather than the other way around.

Later, gripping one of Amy's asscheeks firmly in his left hand, he'll reach under with his right to feel her pussy. The seat beneath and the front flap of the robe will be drenched, aromatic. He'll slide his fingers in easily, brushing aside her labia to stroke her clit, swollen almost to the size of a grape. Spreading her cheeks apart with his free hand, he'll plunge his tongue into her asshole, digging deep, mining the musky depths. "Oh, my god," she'll say. It won't be long before she starts moaning more forcefully and her body convulses and contracts, and then, after one long throaty sigh, she'll relax. Rob will stop then, and after a couple of seconds, test the waters by lightly touching her clit, which will make her fidget and yelp, meaning she's sensitive, she's done.

Earlier, Rob spoke to his parents on the phone. He told them he was staying with a friend until Edie found her own place, and then he'd move back into their apartment. The first part of that was a lie designed to prevent them from worrying about him. They asked if he'd talked to Edie, and he supposed they were hoping he and Edie would still work things out, but he knows that isn't possible. He always thought it was strange that his parents are so normal compared to the parents of other people he grew up around. They're still married to each other, never abused him as a kid, aren't crazy or alcoholic. They are churchgoers, but not zealots. They are neither racists nor champions of civil rights. The one thing they are is silent, and he always suspected they were hiding something underneath all that silence, but whatever that could be remains a mystery even now.

A plastic laundry basket, filled with all the clothes Rob

brought with him when he and Edie separated, is wedged
between captain's chairs and the backseat where Amy's lying
down. A sleeping bag is rolled up and stuffed under that seat as
well. His guitar is in the back wedged next to the spare tire, his
toiletries in the pouch behind the driver's seat, his cell phone in
a cup holder. At night, he often stays in the parking lot of the
bookstore where he works. All he has in the world right now is
within these steel walls.

Later, he'll step over the laundry basket, shift himself around
to the other end of the seat, unzip, and place the tip of his cock
at Amy's lips. She'll put out her tongue, flick blindly. He'll move
his cock farther into her mouth, and she'll close around him as
he grabs the blindfold by the knot at the back to guide her. After
giving her a taste, he'll pull back out, and then he'll repeat the
exercise three or four times—head of the cock on her lips, then
a full immersion, just for a brief couple of seconds. After slip-
ping on a condom, he'll mount her from behind. He'll be excited
enough that a few good thrusts would probably finish him,
but he'll slow himself down, enter her with quiet deliberation.
He'll grind his hips, thinking of a power grinder sparking on
orange-hot iron.

Afterward, he'll pull his pants back up, climb back into the
front seat, and drive away, back to the house where Amy's been
staying. The friends who have been putting her up are conve-
niently out of town tonight.

Rob realizes that he could have driven her almost anywhere
without complaint. He had her full trust and faith. He could
have taken her to Florida, woken her up a few hours later on the
edge of the beach. He could have taken her into the woods, into
the mountains, to another city. Birmingham is not that far from
any number of other environments. But this is where he brought
her: an old steel foundry on a street full of ghosts.

Later, he'll untie her and lead her back into her bed, taking off the blindfold only after she's safely tucked in. They'll sleep until late the next day. In the morning over coffee she'll ask him where he had taken her. Just a parking lot, he'll tell her. A gravel parking lot in a dead part of town.

INDULGENCES

Tenille Brown

George had been caught, literally, red-handed, and he stood there, magazine in hand, red *cock* in hand, staring at Priscilla as if he had never seen her before in his life.

It wasn't that George wasn't allowed to touch himself. It was *his* cock, after all, but they had agreed, *he* had agreed, that he would keep his hands to himself. He would keep them to himself, that was, unless they were on her.

She had only gone to the store. She had spent five minutes at the fucking 7-11 getting a soda and already George had stuffed his hands down his pants and become reacquainted with his cock as if she had been gone for weeks.

Calmly, Priscilla licked her lips. She removed the magazine from George's shaky hands and flipped it open.

There it was, tits and ass everywhere, page after page of breasts and rear ends.

It was typical, typical that George would be drooling after something he already had. As if he didn't live with tits and ass, as if he didn't have complete access to tits and ass every single day.

And like she knew it would, there it came, the pathetic stammering of an explanation.

"I was just having a look and—"

Priscilla placed her hands on her hips. "Yes, George, you were just having a look at the shiny magazine and your hand somehow found its way into your underwear and landed directly on your cock."

She didn't expect a reply. She expected just what he gave her. Shame across his face, chin tucked into his chest, lips folded in embarrassment.

Priscilla didn't waste any time proceeding.

"Well, George," she said. "You've gone and done it. I guess you know what happens now."

And he did. George knew the routine so well that his hands automatically went to the bathroom counter and gripped the edge of the double sink. His long, toned body automatically leaned forward, putting a bend at his waist. He stepped out of the jeans that were already gathered at his ankles and kicked them aside.

George was ready, ass poised, head bent. He was waiting to suffer his repercussions.

Priscilla left him there and went to their bedroom. She shook her head as she flung open her closet door.

It was the seventh time, the seventh time this month she had caught him jerking off. It was the seventh time she'd had to walk to the back of her closet and pull out her leather strap.

She slapped it against her palm now as she headed back toward the bathroom.

Priscilla didn't think she was being unreasonable. Unreasonable would be denying George orgasms, turning her back on him when he reached for her in the middle of the night. But she did none of that. George could come as many times as he wanted.

The deal was, he wouldn't waste any of those times. He wouldn't rub and jerk into his hands what could be, what rightfully *should* be inside of her.

And it wasn't that he didn't fuck her, that he preferred the palm of his hand to the inside of her cunt. He fucked her regularly and he fucked her well.

The thing was, Priscilla was thirty-eight and she didn't have the time to waste for George to be coming inside his boxers like some horny teenager.

A deal was a deal. Still, George had given in to this indulgence of his, and since *he* had indulged, *she* would indulge.

But Priscilla's indulgence didn't involve flipping open a magazine and touching herself. Standing in the doorway of the bathroom, she cleared her throat. Yes, Priscilla's indulgence involved touching George.

She approached him, stopping only when she stood a few steps behind him.

Her arm drawn back, hand high over her head, Priscilla gave her final words: "I certainly hope it was worth it, George."

She didn't wait for him to respond before she brought her hand down with such force that the strap caused a whipping sound in the air. Shortly after came the crack of leather making contact with flesh.

The pink skin on George's ass rippled with the first strike. His muscular thighs clenched. Priscilla knew without looking that he was gritting his teeth, squeezing his eyes shut.

Priscilla spoke. "Now, tell me again, George, why we don't jerk off all willy-nilly around here."

Strike.

George rose up on the balls of his feet, his toes gripping the carpet.

His voice was a throaty whisper. "Because, Priscilla, there is a plan."

Priscilla nodded. She whacked him again with less intensity, but still hard enough for him to throw his head back in agony.

She said, "And that plan is?"

She stopped long enough to await his answer.

Breathless, George said, "To give you a...so that we can have..."

Priscilla grew impatient. "To get me knocked up, right?"

George nodded. "Right." He tucked his chin, and Priscilla couldn't tell if he were wincing or smiling.

Nevertheless, Priscilla knew she had done enough. She walked out of the bathroom and put her strap away.

It was probably a waste, anyway. After all, who knew how many times George *didn't* get caught, how many times he had whacked off and finished just seconds before Priscilla walked through the door? She was being easy on him, really, giving him the benefit of the doubt, issuing punishment for only crimes she had witnessed with her own eyes.

Yet somehow it calmed her, this indulgence of hers, made her feel better that she could control at least some aspect of her life. And with that comfort, she left George to replace his clothing and went to the kitchen to pour her soda over ice.

It shouldn't have surprised her, the news. That was her shitty luck, after all.

Now, safely inside her front door, Priscilla pulled the cup out of her purse, the plastic, medicinal cup that would measure her husband's juice and count up the chances she would have of ever having a baby.

George walked into the living room, already dressed for work.

"You left early," he said.

Priscilla shrugged, tossing her long, dark hair across her shoulder. "Had to be there early."

George's eyes fell on the cup. "Whatcha got there?"

Priscilla slid it over to him. "It's your new best friend," she said.

He cocked his head. "Excuse me?"

"That's right. It's your come catcher. They want to count your boys down at the clinic."

George began his familiar nervous stutter. "I can't do that... not in that."

Priscilla rolled her eyes. "I had a feeling you might say that. So, I stopped by the store on my way home."

She pulled the glossy magazine out of her purse and tossed it onto the coffee table.

She watched for George's reaction, waited to see in his eyes what she saw every time she walked into the bathroom and caught him gripping his cock.

When George remained silent, Priscilla spoke. "Now you listen to me. This is the only time I will allow this. This is the only time this will be acceptable, until after, well, you know."

She pushed the magazine in George's direction.

George shook his head. "And I'm just supposed to do it, just like that?"

Priscilla threw up her hands. "You do it all the time, George, what's the difference?"

He tucked his lips and furrowed his brow.

"Look," she said. "There's nothing to be embarrassed about. Just go on in the bathroom like you normally do. Close the door and act like I'm not even here. Just give me a shout when you're done, and I'll run it back up to the office."

George nodded. Slowly, he picked up the cup and tucked the

magazine under his arm. He disappeared around the corner.

Priscilla sat on the couch and watched the morning news for the next fifteen minutes. When twenty minutes passed, she rose. George could have finished twice by now.

She tapped softly on the bathroom door before she pushed it open.

"Everything okay in here?" she asked.

George held the still empty cup in his hands. His fly was undone; his cock was exposed and flaccid.

"It isn't working," George said. "It never works unless I know you're close by."

Priscilla folded her arms. "But I'm ten steps away."

George shook his head. "That's not what I mean. I need for you to...well, I want..."

And then, just like that, it became clear as a bell.

Priscilla's voice was soft, almost a whisper. "You need for me to *catch* you, George?"

George nodded, as if giving voice to the notion would validate it as ridiculous.

Priscilla nodded slowly, exhaling.

She left the room. She waited five minutes and returned.

And, like clockwork, George's face was red when she opened the door, the magazine was in front of him, and his cock was hard in his hand.

Priscilla leaned against the doorframe.

"Well, George," she said. "It looks like, once again, I've caught you. But, I'm going to be nice about it this time. I'm going to let you finish." Priscilla tilted her head toward the cup.

George hung his head. "I can't," he said.

Priscilla raised her eyebrows. "You *still* can't?"

"No, I can't finish, until you..." His voice drifted off.

And with the snap of sudden realization, Priscilla stood up

straight. Without a word, she went to their bedroom, entered her closet and retrieved her favorite leather strap.

George was in position when she returned.

She raised her hand high above her head and brought the strap down on his awaiting ass. Steadily and soundly, she spanked him.

Priscilla struck George with the strap until sweat sprang from her temples. She struck him until the sight between his legs caused her to stop.

All this time, Priscilla had been sure George was thinking about something else, something, anything, other than her spanking him. She was sure he was thinking about all the tits and ass he had been feasting his eyes upon, since usually, after only three strikes, his cock would rise.

But now Priscilla knew. She knew why George was always so hesitant to turn around when she was done. As if he couldn't face her, couldn't bear to associate his hard-on with her punishment.

And while pleasing George had never been Priscilla's intention, she became wet at the sight of his rigid cock.

"Turn around, George. Let me get a good view of what you've got there," she said.

George obeyed. His hard-on extended out in front of him.

"Interesting," Priscilla said. "Now, however did that happen? I mean, surely you weren't thinking of those girls in the magazine when you were getting your ass spanked?"

She didn't wait for an answer.

"Go on. You can finish now," she said, holding the cup in front of him.

And when George rose up on his feet and his face and ass flushed rosy pink and he filled the cup to the line, Priscilla knew that some indulgences were, sometimes, worth allowing.

LOGAN

Rosalind Christine Lloyd

I had the biggest crush on my friend Logan. She was truly one of the coolest chicks I knew. This made things at home a little crazy since she happened to be my roommate and I happen to be a lesbian. Roommate crushes suck.

She was this tiny little thing, you might call it petite. Petite as she was though, she was, literally, all tits and all ass. I don't mean this with any kind of disrespect, but Logan was a voluptuous balance of womanhood that turned the heads of both men and women. She rocked this radical sense of style. The deep burgundy-colored dred faux-hawk was just a little shocking, and she had this amazing tribal tattoo that looked Celtic or African. It started at the nape of her neck, stretching itself across her shoulders, around her arms, and crawling down her back, working itself all the way down to her nether regions. It was an amazing work of art, much of it I'd not had the pleasure of viewing in its entirety.

Although Logan had a knack for wearing as little clothing

as possible to showcase her worldly goods, I always felt like I needed to see even more of her. Logan designed funky pottery for a living, and much of it hung out in any free corner of our apartment. Her claim to fame was having sold some of her pieces to a few New York–based celebrities. She taught pottery classes in Williamsburg where her technique was so popular there was a waitlist just to be in her company. Watching her at work, her tiny little hands molding wet clay, was a sight for sore eyes. And with these same hands she used to talk. Because when she spoke, she barely opened her mouth, with a clenched jaw, almost as if she was talking to herself. I don't think she liked talking very much, only when necessary. And it was usually laced with some profanity. A pack of American Spirits seemed to grow out of her left hand, if she wasn't working clay, or talking. But she was brilliant. Many people told her so. She moved in with me to save up cash to buy her own working studio/living space.

Now Logan had been informed, by me of course, about my crush and her gentle response continued to be, "I love you Angel, but I am hopelessly, strictly dick-ly. There is not a dildo or a chick's vagina, a tongue, or touch in this entire universe that could convert me. But that doesn't mean I don't respect your swagger. Girl Power! Hell fuckin' yeah." Point taken. But not like she needed to remind me. I just checked in with her from time to time. Besides, I couldn't argue, as I have very similar opinions about being positively about the pussy, nothing but the pussy.

This brings me to her boyfriend, Jack. Jack was pretty cool. He was this dark, skinny dude with sad blue eyes and a different skateboard for every day of the week, although oddly he had no means of employment to speak of. I never asked about it. For some reason, I could have sworn Logan had told Jack I had a crush on her, though she patently denied it. But I honestly didn't think he gave a shit anyway. His fashion sense, or lack thereof, his being a vegan, and his taste in music were all lost on me. The only thing he and I had in common was an infinite desire for pussy. He was at our place a lot and he never came empty handed. He'd always bring over some veggie takeout, plenty of beer, and even some trees, which he always offered to me. By the end of the night, I could hear him fucking the hell out of Logan in her bedroom, heat emanating from the wall separating our rooms like I was living right next to hell. They were extremely vocal about their pleasuring of each other, with moans and groans that would push against the air and into my room and into my ears. Automatically I would touch myself because, frankly, it was hard not to be aroused by it. Really hard.

One weekend I had to go out of town to visit some friends in Miami. On the way to the airport, I had a feeling my trip was doomed by the way the storm clouds hovered over the New York City skyline. The minute I stepped out of the taxi, rain came thundering angrily down and did not stop for the next three hours. Seeing as this was the last flight out of JFK that night, I knew my weekend was screwed. The usual game plan was that my friends would pick me up from Miami International and we'd hit the clubs immediately thereafter, but that wasn't going to happen. My flight was canceled, and so was my South Beach party weekend.

Totally irritated, I grabbed a taxi back home while the storm raged on. When I got there, the apartment was fairly dark but for the tiny tea lights everywhere that lit the living room like glittering stars. They were my tea lights; Logan often helped herself to my stuff because I was such a pushover for her. Some of my girlfriends and jump-offs hated this about me. Walking inside, I could hear this really crazy music playing in the background. I knew it had to be something that Jack had chosen or maybe even created himself. He was not a musician or poet, and yet he always wrote these corny love songs and poems filled with longing to Logan. Who could blame him? If Logan Williams were mine, I would do all kinds of crazy shit just to keep her happy, too. Just to see her smile. Just to hear her squeal with delight or moan with ecstasy. Yep, Jack was one lucky guy.

Back to the candles. So it would seem that I was walking into something. And that something was in the middle of the living room. Logan was bent over a chair, completely naked except for a blindfold, her ass raised high in the air, her hands tied to either arm of the chair. I was actually able to see just how intricately awesome her tattoo was. It was a massive thing, a dizzying design that must have taken forever to ink, a design that traveled all the way down to the base of her spine, the gnarly vine morphing into a tiny serrated tail. The end of it disappeared into the crack of her glorious-sized ass. My heart stopped when I noticed what made her ass look so plump and appealing. She was wearing my five-inch black patent leather Christian Louboutins. Not my Christian Louboutins! How long had she been standing there like that? The whole scene put me in a state of confusion. The rain, the strange dark music, the candles, and my current little obsession standing there in front of me in the most vulnerable, submissive state, wearing my favorite shoes! What was I supposed to do? I was moving to approach her when she called out.

"Jack? Come on, darling. If you weren't so cheap you'd have a box of rubbers here instead of always rushing out to buy them two at a time!"

I just froze. And waited to see if Jack answered. When he didn't, I moved again, closer to her.

"Jack?" she called again. "Stop playing around and get busy! Can't you see I'm moist standing here waiting for you? You need to hurry and beat this bum up."

It was a golden moment I couldn't bear to pass up. I put my hands together in prayer, thanking the Goddess Lesbos for this gift of opportunity, rubbing my now-sweaty palms together before reeling back and spanking the tender sweet ass of Logan Williams.

"Oh, yes. That's what I'm talking about, you beautiful motherfucker. That's what I've been waiting for." I could hardly believe my ears. She sounded so sweet, I needed to hear her speak again. Kissing the palm of my right hand, I swung it back again, this time like a Williams sister at some "open" before slamming it again into the flesh of her soft, sweet ass.

"Damn it, yes, bitch. Again! Yes, you fuckin' naughty bitch. You can do better than that. I know you can. Come on. Again!" Logan usually had a confident tone to her voice, but I was impressed with this side of her I didn't know. She and Jack had a hotter sex life than I'd thought.

Seeing her in my shoes, all six inches (think one hundred dollars per inch) of them and looking at her exposed, gorgeous, golden ass, the ass that she was giving to ol' Jack, well, I got jealous. And this jealously provoked me to charge into a relentless but well-paced spanking of her ass with my bare right hand that left me a little winded—and Logan very much in appreciation. I think it gave the impression I knew what I was doing and with every slap, Logan would raise that little ass even higher to meet my hand in the spot she wanted it. With every slap her butt got warmer and warmer to the touch as did my hand.

I developed a nice, even pace, each spank sending all kinds of crazy erotic messages to my brain I couldn't decipher. At some point, my hand started to tingle. Urging me on each time my hand connected with her butt, her potty mouth continued saying shit that kept me hard and dripping in my tight jeans. I stepped back for a moment, walking around her slowly until I faced her. Staring at her blindfolded face, I looked at her long nose and tiny, puckered lips, which conveyed anticipation mixed with wanting.

"What are you doing?" she asked. "You better finish what you started. My muscles are beginning to throb, baby. You need to do something about this." She moved her body forward a little against the chair, raising one luscious leg to scratch the other with the nasty point of the shoe. I couldn't resist the urge to trace the designs of her tattoo with my index finger, dragging it slowly and gently toward the bump of her behind.

"You like my tat-a-tat-tat, don't you?" I nodded my head affirmatively as I walked back behind her, hand still on her butt. I needed a closer look. Kneeling down, I was front and center, audience to Logan Williams's juicy pussy and the tiny knot of her ass. Only lit by candlelight, seeing it up close and personal was sheer gynecological magic. It felt warm near my face, the layers of pink flesh like moist living silk. The bulb of her clit almost looked creamy. I'd gotten this far, and I wasn't about to hold back. I traced my index finger right in between her lips. Logan sucked in air between her teeth and moaned. Sticking my finger in deeper, I felt my desire grow into a bit of a monster I had to control. Logan wiggled around me while I spread her lips with my fingers. I leaned in deeper, trying to look inside her. Smelling her made me want to taste her. I almost did. Sliding my finger up farther to her little love knot, I spread her cheeks open with one hand and with the other hand, using the tip of my index finger, I started a repetitious tapping of her anus that made her cheeks quiver.

"Fuck!" Logan hissed. "Fuck me now, bitch. I want your thick, pink cock in there. Right there." If I only had a cock.

My hand was stinging, and not being blessed with ambidexterity, I found myself searching the room to help us along. And there, by the door, was one of Jack's latest contraptions of a skateboard. Longer, wider, and flatter than your average skateboard, it had these small sets of wheels that swiveled. Interesting. And nicely painted. I thought the deep fluorescent purple might look quite nice in the candlelight, as I wanted to create the same shade on Logan's ass. I was running on pure adrenalin at this point. If my actions seemed a little risky, at least I recognized I was coasting on some kind of crazy good luck.

"What are you contemplating, J? You're taking too long a break. My ass is waiting." Logan talked a lot of shit. And I couldn't say anything. I couldn't ask her if she liked it. I couldn't taste her, I couldn't fuck her, I couldn't have her. If I gave myself away it would be the end of it. And there I was, opportunity teasing me, screwing around with my head. Naked before me in the middle of our living room, blindfolded and tied to a chair, her delicate toes gracing the insides of my favorite shoes, her beautiful ass raised high in the air. I had left any sense of my integrity at the door.

Yeah, I felt like shit. But I couldn't take anything back. Not a fuckin' thing. And the thought of this made me whack her hard with that skateboard, landing just underneath her ass on the meaty part of her thighs. She cried out this time, without a saucy backup line to follow. The cry teetered between pleasure and pain, the perfect balance of both. I needed to do it again. Swinging the board up high, I aimed at the dead center of her buttocks and caught it just right. This caused the entire chair to move, and the flesh on her ass sprang back and forth again. A rush of air escaped from Logan's lungs. The wheels went spinning on the skateboard, the ball bearings mimicking the raindrops that sprinkled against the windows.

"Uhmmm," she moaned. "What the fuck is that? Shit, damn, that's good," she said.

Her bum was now a hot pink, and the folds of her pussy and the nub of her clit looked as if they were on fire. I knew that I was failing miserably at this test of respect and restraint. This reality had only provoked me to develop a firmer grip on the skateboard before spanking her again with it, when the room was suddenly invaded by harsh bright light coming from the hallway. It was Jack. He looked at me standing there behind his girl, his skateboard in my hands. I just froze. He looked at my jacket, which was dripping wet just like his. He glanced at my luggage that sat on the other side of the door. Time stopped for just a few seconds. Then this smile crept its way onto his face. Pressing his index finger against his lips and winking, he quietly tiptoed over to us. He held that same finger up, motioning to me, then pointing to Logan's juicy red ass. He was indicating that I should spank her one more time. His dick had to be just as hard as my clit; shit, as hard as Logan's clit. I didn't hesitate. When I spanked her, aiming for her ass and for her lovely swollen flower, she squealed blissfully.

"Oh, Jack, I love you, you fuckin' prick. Give it to me again. Please, baby. Come on." Jack and I both laughed silently, for different reasons maybe. I handed him the skateboard, which he accepted after giving me the thumbs-up, as if to say, *Great idea*. I went into the kitchen to pour all three of us double shots of bourbon. I deposited two of the glasses on the table next to Jack and Logan and took mine into my room. For some reason, I found a new appreciation for Jack's music as the lovely Logan wailed not so eloquently in the background.

DADDY'S GIRL

Teresa Noelle Roberts

Daddy strides into the living room, between me and the TV, and switches off the "Buffy" rerun I'm halfheartedly watching.

Then he holds up a pack of cigarettes and a romance novel. "I found these in your room, Cherise. What do you have to say for yourself?"

Heart pounding like a techno track, palms wet and mouth dry, I plaster on a brassy, totally fake smile. "You always tell me I should read more?"

I squeak at the end.

Damn it. He's caught me by surprise, and it's making me nervous.

"Smut isn't what I had in mind."

"It's just a romance novel, Daddy." I knew the cigarettes would get me in trouble, but I'm surprised he's harping on the book. He's always got his nose in a book—sometimes some classic, since he's a lit professor, but just as likely a thriller, and he knows I love a good romance as much as he loves a good save-the-world-from-the-bad-guys adventure.

Maybe the difference is that this is an *erotic* romance, and a kinky one at that?

I jump up and try to snatch the book away from him, but it's too late. He opens it at my bookmark, and begins to read out loud in a rich voice, like he's reading Shakespeare.

Oh, god. It's the part where the hero gives the heroine a sexy spanking. Hearing Daddy read it is so embarrassing.

Embarrassing, yet hot.

My face burns, and I squirm from humiliation and horniness, pressing my thighs closer together as if that would protect my clit from being attacked by lust.

Instead, it gets me excited.

It's not just what he's reading. What's getting to me is *him* reading it, with his deep whisky voice and the blue eyes behind the sexy-professor horn-rims, and the way he's disapproving and disdainful and amused all at once.

A girl's Daddy shouldn't read her things like that, in that way. It's just not what fathers do.

He's not playing by the rules, not following the script.

It's freaking me out and it's turning me on and it's freaking me out because it's turning me on.

He stops reading just as the characters move on from spanking to screwing. "What do you have to say for yourself, young woman? Doesn't that sound foolish, read aloud?" He's not just scolding me. He's making fun of me, too. Great.

I roll my eyes. "Daddy, it's just a book. I like it, and besides, Tom Clancy would sound just as dumb if I did a dramatic reading."

He takes a step forward, and then another, taking over my personal space. I'm surrounded by his cologne, the leathery-woodsy one that's like Essence of Grown Man, and I know I ought to back away, but instead I've grown roots into the rug.

"You're right about Tom Clancy," he admits. "But if you want to read about erotic spanking, let me find you something better. I doubt this author has been spanked since she was six years old and got caught stealing cookies."

God, what am I supposed to say to that? He's so not playing by the rules, so not acting like a proper Daddy, and I can't keep up. And I actually thought she'd done a pretty good job with the spanking scene, so that's pissing me off a little.

I thought my face was burning before, but he's thrown napalm on it. And apparently some of it got into my panties, because things are on fire down there. I finally manage to spit out, "That's gross."

"You're reading that tripe and you're talking to me about gross?"

Tripe? Who the hell actually says that anymore? I almost ask him that, but his nearness, the smell of his cologne, the throbbing between my legs, all conspire to tie my tongue.

And that gives him enough time to make his move.

One hand brings the offending trade paperback down on my butt with a surprisingly firm thud. The other grabs my ponytail, uses it to propel me forward.

He forces my mouth against his. I keep my lips firmly shut.

He keeps smacking me with the book as he kisses me.

I fight it for as long as I can—fight the seductive stinging against my ass, fight the mixture of arousal and alarm flooding me. Finally, my lips open, and I melt against him and let him plunder my mouth. He's hard against my bare thigh, and that's killing me. I want to rub myself against it, but that's just not what a girl does to her Daddy.

"I think," Daddy says, "that you need to be punished—to know what a proper spanking feels like so you'll know when you're reading bad porn. Don't you agree, Cherise?"

I pretend to consider the question. My face is scarlet, I can tell, and my white cotton hipster panties are soaked through, and even though things have gotten weird, I know what answer is expected of me. "I've been a bad girl, Daddy. I deserve to be punished."

I look contrite and nervous. He looks stern and annoyed, but eager at the same time.

Then we both start laughing—first him, then me, laughing and holding each other, his hard body pressed against me. His lips press against my hair, and he whispers, still chuckling, "I love you."

We both rearrange our faces appropriately, he to the stern father, I to the nervous teenager. I wonder if it's as hard for him as it is for me.

He sits on the sofa, pulls me roughly over his knee. "Daddy, please..." I protest. It sounds more like I'm begging for him to give me the spanking I crave.

Which is true. Very little here is what it seems.

"Daddy" is my lover, Mike, not my father. My name isn't Cherise, either; it's Kaitlyn. The fake name helps me separate. Otherwise I don't think I could let myself indulge in these punishment fantasies, let alone the semi-incestuous ones. It's a trick I learned from the ex-boyfriend who lured me into his kinky world of spanking and erotic role-play, and one I've taught Mike.

I'd never let myself be spanked before I learned that trick. I had too much trouble letting go of my real-life doctor self, and all its responsibilities, to indulge my spanking-and-discipline fantasies. Making it all a game, with the spanker and spankee both characters, allows me to have my fun without giving up any real power or control. Besides, I like the whole package: the role-play, the costumes, the way it lets us toy with taboos without actually violating them.

Only today it's all going a bit oddly.

At this point I should be deep into role-playing teenage Cherise, scared because she's in trouble and because her Daddy's crossing lines that fathers shouldn't cross. To make it worse for her, Cherise thinks her Dad's a Hot Older Man, the kind she'd have fantasies about if he was someone else's father, and wrong as it is, she's getting turned on. It's a game we've played often before, and it always works.

But right now I'm thrown. Excited, but thrown. Mike's deviated from the script. He was supposed to "find" and react to the cigarettes, not the novel.

Bringing the book into it is getting too close to reality for my taste. I don't want to feel like Mike's spanking me for something that bugs him in real life—and while it doesn't make sense that he'd suddenly be offended by my taste in novels, I'm not sure why else he'd bring the book into it.

Of course, my brain's not working at one hundred percent right now because the blood that's supposed to power it has rushed to my clit. I'm easy to confuse in this state.

We're not following the script anymore, the script that keeps my fantasies safe. But even though my head's in a bit of an uproar, I'm still wet and still eager to have Mike—Daddy, I mean—paddle my ass.

He flips up my short plaid skirt. Runs his hand over my cotton-clad ass. I force myself to squirm away, but I'm sure he can tell I'm rubbing myself against him, not trying to escape.

"You've been bad, Cherise. I'm going to spank your bare bottom, like the heroine in that appalling book." It sounds so corny that I can't help laughing, although I try to disguise it with a groan.

I want to remind him he groans over some of the writing in some of his thrillers and still gets sucked into the story—but I'm afraid if I do, I'll blow the mood, blow being Cherise, miss out on my spanking.

He hooks his fingers in the elastic waistband of my panties. As Cherise, I should be struggling and protesting, but instead I raise my hips and wiggle to make it easier for him to yank them down. Sometimes it's hard to make myself fight back when I want it this badly.

Then I spread my legs so he can see how wet I am.

I know Mike wants to touch, but he's not Mike now, he's Daddy, and Daddy just chuckles deep in his throat. "Poor little girl. That's what happens when you read too much smut."

He plants one hand on the back of my head to keep me in place.

The other one starts spanking.

Sometimes he starts off hard and fast, going for a sharp build to crescendo. This time, he opens soft and sensual, little teasing pats that make me want to purr, that bring the blood to my asscheeks gradually. I raise my butt, eager for more, and he gives me more, going faster and harder, building a rhythm.

Soon, my ass feels huge and hot and tender, but in a good way, like huge and hot and tender is its proper state, and I've been waiting for years, not knowing what I was missing, for someone to repair my sad unspanked bottom. My entire body tingles, alive and excited by the smacks on my ass, the firm, controlling hand on the back of my head. I can't get away, I don't want to get away, I want to lie forever over Mike's lap as his hand smacks down on my ass and thighs.

No. Daddy's lap. Mike doesn't spank me.

Mike's lap? Daddy's lap?

Hell, I'm not sure who I am at the moment. Cherise and Kaitlyn blur together into a creature of pure sensation who just wants to enjoy this wonderful spanking.

Every time his hand smacks down, I rise up to meet it. Every time he lifts his hand again, I grind my bare mound as best I can against his corduroy-covered thigh. It's a slow build, each slap and each grind getting me closer to orgasm without pushing me over the edge.

Close. So close.

The room's gone. My mind is gone. There's nothing left in this world but my throbbing ass and my straining, swollen clit, and Daddy's hand, Daddy's body, the smell of Daddy surrounding me, Daddy's voice telling me what a naughty, naughty girl I am.

But when the orgasm takes me, throws me even farther from normal reality, forces a scream from my throat, what I cry out isn't "Daddy!" but "Mike!"

He pulls me up, helps me sit on his lap. Every ridge of the corduroy is an exquisite torture to my sore butt. I wrap my arms around his neck and cuddle close, feeling small and safe and very much loved.

As I start to come down from the heights, I realize I'd called him by the "wrong" name, try to recover with "I love you, Daddy."

He kisses the top of my head. "I think I liked it better when you called me Mike. Maybe we can save Cherise and Daddy for special occasions and just be you and me when I spank you."

I go from warm and fuzzy to anxious in a heartbeat, not sure I like where he's going. He notices, I think, because he kisses me so sweetly and deeply that my body turns to liquid. Then he slips his hand between my thighs and with a few flicks of his finger on my already sensitive clit, liquid becomes light and I'm flying again.

This is something that Daddy never does to Cherise. Cherise may get off on being spanked, and Daddy may say and do things that would be inappropriate for a real father, but he never does anything directly sexual. Caressing me is for Mike, not Daddy.

So is fucking me, and when he lifts me up so he can unzip his pants and take out his cock, I think that I could get used to Mike rather than Daddy doing the spanking if it ends like this.

After he pulls me down to straddle his cock, filling me like I didn't know I ached to be filled, he starts smacking my tender ass. This time there's no doubt at all who's doing the spanking because his cock is deep inside me and my eyes are locked into his and he's saying my own name. This time, when I shudder and scream, it's with Mike.

Yum. Spanking and fucking, two great tastes that taste great together, far better than peanut butter and chocolate. It's just... it's just not something I've ever let myself do before. My ex liked to keep it separate, and it was easier, safer, that way.

He feels my body tense, asks me what's wrong. I sort through a few variations before finding the right words. "That was great. But I don't want you punishing me. That's what Daddy's for—so it's not real and I can enjoy the spanking."

I didn't think he could pull me any closer, but he manages to. "Kaitlyn, sweetheart, you know this isn't punishment. It's fun. Sometimes I'd rather just be me, spanking the woman I love."

"But...the book. You were scolding me. I don't like that."

"Oh, shit, you weren't supposed to take that seriously! That was part of the game."

Then he makes a weird face. "Besides, I picked that one off the bedside table because the cover picture was sexy and...well, the next thing I knew it was three hours later."

"Ha! Told you they were addictive!"

He goes on. He loves to talk about books. "I loved the bit you'd bookmarked because the heroine was so open about liking to be spanked—and the hero is like me, loving how much it turns her on. I wanted to read it out loud during our scene, but

I couldn't figure out how to do it and still sound like Daddy."

I feel a weight sink off me and through the floor. Now that we've tried it, I'd like good clean spanky fun mixed with fucking on a more regular basis, and I think I can even admit that now.

But a bit of me is disappointed. When an ER doctor has a bad day at work, it's *really* bad. I want to make everything better, to save everyone, to get the world back under control, and I can't. When I get home after a day like that, shucking being a grown-up and being bratty Cherise taken in hand by Daddy is exactly what I need.

It isn't easy for me to say so in as many words, but after several false starts, I manage to get it out.

"That makes sense, Kaitlyn. I love spanking you because it's fun and turns you on, but I definitely see why being Cherise is good for you sometimes—and I like that you like it." He changes his voice to the stern Daddy-voice. "And young lady, if you start acting up, and especially if I catch you with cigarettes, your Daddy is going to punish you!"

And what I say to that, since I'm not Cherise at the moment, is "Yum!"

THE DEPTHS OF DESPAIR

Rachel Kramer Bussel

Evan is staring at me intently, waiting for the answer to his question, "What do you want?" whispered directly into my ear. Such a short sentence for the very complex response it opens up in me. I want a hundred million things from him, but at this moment, I want something I'm not totally sure either of us can handle.

"I want you to make me cry," I tell him. I have to whisper it because the words, and the realization, are so intense I'm not sure I can own up to them. But it's true; every time I think about his hands crashing down on me, his words berating me, his power keeping me in my lowly place, things we've done hundreds of times but that I still clamor for, I realize I don't want something light and easy, something we can laugh about later. I don't even want compliments like, "God, you can take a lot." It's not a competition for me; I know what my body can do, but I want to see what we can do together, if we can take spanking somewhere it's never gone before, if we can make it propel us into a new place where we lose ourselves only to find people we've always wanted to be. I've wanted this forever, I realize, as I say the words, but had never felt close enough with a lover to go there before him. I want something altogether different from every other spanking I've ever gotten, the ones that were hot and kinky and nasty, but that shied away from even approaching the edge of oblivion. Only with Evan can I dare to approach that dividing line that could topple our over-the-knee pleasures forever, or consecrate spanking as the centerpiece of our relationship.

I've never had to use a safeword before, and most of the time, I've barely even had one I could use. I trust my lovers implicitly and have never felt the need for one. Buried within that trust, though, is a safety net I'm not sure I any longer want, a safety net that suddenly feels altogether too constricting. I've never liked the word *play* used to describe kink, or at least, my kink. There's nothing playful about it, even though I know all about safe, sane, and consensual, and that I can stop at any time. I can top from below with the best of them, but something in me has finally rebelled at this topsy-turvy state of masochistic affairs. I'm ready for the real thing, and am finally strong enough to take it, and Evan is just the man to grant me my wish.

If we were the marrying kind, I'd have a nice, shiny rock to flash around to all and sundry. We're not, so I don't expect that, but I married him in my heart a month after we met. He had his cock inside me, was fucking me doggie-style, and I moved, just slightly, almost imperceptibly. "Don't move, Denise. Don't ever move. Stay with me forever," he said. I could've dismissed it as pillow talk, most women would have, but somehow I knew he meant it. We've had our ups and downs in the year we've been together, but I've always known that he was the one. Not the One, the mystical, magical, phantom lover meant to fulfill a woman's every need and fantasy before she can even think of them. Not that One, but this one, my special one, the one who makes my heart beat like we're on a crashing airplane, who makes me smile when he wakes me in the middle of the night with a particularly loud snore, the one whose eyes and cock compete for best feature. The one who's made me relearn what submission is all about.

Yet even after a year of me naked over his knee, or up against the wall, or bent over holding my ankles, or any number of other positions we've tried to perfect our spanking regimen, we still haven't reached the heights, or depths, I know we could. I haven't cracked the surface of his sadism, haven't pushed him to bring out the truly mean top I know lurks inside, haven't let myself sink into the glory of sub space so fully I wonder if I'll ever come out. My fantasies have gotten more and more twisted, perverse, unreal. But I don't want an army of lovers or community-wide kink; I want Evan, just Evan. It's through no fault of his, or mine, that we haven't gone there, I've just always surrendered to the lure of his cock when the pressure seemed unbearable, right before I went over the edge I'm afraid I'll never return from. What if after this I want him to make me cry all the time? What if he takes that as a sign I need therapy? What if we become one of those couples where the man gets off on fucking his wife but not in the way that makes him rush home to her? What if he thinks I'm crying because I'm sad or in pain or don't love him anymore? I have no answers or crystal ball, I only know that the tears are demanding an exit, and won't take no for an answer. They aren't tears of sadness, that much I know for sure; what these tears signify I don't yet know, but I am convinced Evan can help me understand.

He grabs me by the scruff of my neck, and I whimper, just like I have before, but there's something different in his eyes.

They're feral, wild with a kind of desire I've never seen before, and that sight unleashes a wave of want inside me. My entire body goes tight, then limp. "Be careful what you wish for, Dee," he says. "Very, very careful." When I make a move to open my mouth, he shuts my lips, pressing them between his thumb and forefinger. "Don't speak until we're done. You'll know when we're done. You can make noise, scream all you want, but no talking, unless you need to safeword. Your safeword is *emergency*. But I don't think you're going to come anywhere close to using it." He lets go of my lips, then just stands there staring at me. At an even six feet, he's got a good five inches on me so I'm looking at up him, my face just as serious as his.

Then, in a flash, he's grabbed me and moved us over so he can slam me against the wall. This is no gentle crash in which I'm just as complicit; *he* slams *me,* and it hurts, but I like the pain. A lot. My face smashes into the familiar white space, his hand against the side of my head. I've been up against countless walls since I met him, but never so close, where it's like I'm inhaling the paint. I've murmured, prayed even, into wood and brick and paint. But now my lips aren't so much touching the wall as merged with it. My body goes on red alert as he smears me into the wall. My pussy is pounding, demanding attention in much the same way my heart is thudding. "Stay there, whore." He knows that word sets me off, but this time, his voice is gruffer; it's not a playful term of endearment, and I almost feel like one. I wonder what I'd do if I really were a whore with a client who wanted to treat me like this. I focus on the plaster against my skin, on his hand that has just stabbed me in the lower back. Okay, not stabbed, but the pressure there is exquisite, his palm digging into the spot where my back curves, his thumb resting against my anus.

Then his hand booms down against my right buttcheek. I'd

thought I couldn't sink farther into the wall, but I'd been wrong, because somehow, I become one with it. It hurts, and not in the way my ass does. My facial pain isn't quite the sweet, stinging, arousing pain that spanking brings, but this pain still manages to feel good in its own way, reminding me what I'm capable of in the name of getting off. I know my face will be red later, probably my breasts, too. His hand keeps coming down against me, spanking me furiously in a way that surely has to singe his palm as much as it does my bottom. Then his teeth are sinking into the back of my neck and his four fingers are turning the backs of my thighs red. "Denise, now's as good a time as any to tell you. It's over." He's spanking me hard the whole time he speaks, and the smacks are so loud I almost can't make out what he's saying. "I didn't know how to break it to you, but I'm moving out. I've found my own place, over on Larch. I've got two more weeks here, and I'll try to be as discreet as I can. I was waiting for the right time to tell you, but now's as good as any, wouldn't you say?" He's talking like we're having some kind of adult conversation, while meanwhile my entire stomach has dropped, yet my pussy is still on fire.

So is my ass, where he's still spanking me. I've had my hands up above me on the wall, but they start to drop. All I want now is to curl into a ball, wrapped around myself. *Fuck spanking,* I think, about to whisper, "Emergency," when he presses his entire body against mine, lifting my hands back above me and pressing his palms to the backs of my hands, hard. "Keep those there, Dee. I said two more weeks, and don't think I'm not gonna get the most pussy out of you I can before then. I don't want to forget this ass," he says as he pinches the skin there.

I'm not crying; I'm numb inside. Did I bring this on? This wasn't what I wanted. I keep my hands above me just to spite him. Now I won't cry, just to show him. "Stay right fucking there. Whore," he says, and despite myself, I feel a shudder. He knows why it triggers me so: I used to be one, at least the worst kind of one, one who gave it away to anyone who so much as looked my way, succumbing to the word I'd been called since sprouting 38Ds in my senior year of high school yet it also thrills a deep, secret place inside me. I was a slut who was so far gone she thought of herself as a whore, and even got off on the blasé way I could pick a guy up, bring him home, and chuck him out the door. But that nameless blur of men and cocks was nothing compared to the power I tapped into with Evan. Even the good guys, the ones trained in the art of BDSM, who worshipped my ass as much as they punished it, couldn't come close to what we have. Had. I don't know anymore. His hands are everywhere at once, firing off blows that make my whole body light up in recognition of my place, my role in this apocalyptic scene. I briefly wonder if he'll offer me money that I have to take from him with my teeth, as one guy did when I did a brief stint stripping. Yet even with his horrific words ringing in my ear, the image makes me wet. I picture him shoving dollar bills into my cunt, into my mouth, gluing them to my body, marking me as a whore once and for all.

My mind goes a little quieter as he slips the blindfold over my eyes. "Get over here," he says, grabbing me by my nipple, pinching it as he pulls me across the room. The point where our bodies touch stings, but a soothing, familiar heat travels lower. *I've asked for this, I want this, we'll deal with the aftermath later,* I think, as I feel him bend me over the spanking bench we bought in our first heady, kinky weeks together. *Who will spank me on it when he leaves?* I wonder as he settles me over it so my ass is perfectly poised. I expect the spanking to start up again immediately, and perhaps because of that, it doesn't. I can't see, but I can hear him moving around, the flick of a lighter, the sharp inhale of a cigarette. I don't approve, but I gave up lecturing him long ago.

"You'll be rid of this smell soon enough," he says, as if reading my mind. He blows hot smoke against my ass, and I tremble. I'm waiting, patiently, if you ask me, but he just strokes my asscheeks with the tips of his fingers, tickling me more than anything else. "I'll miss this ass, Denise. I hope you believe me. It just has to be this way."

"Is it Monique?" I ask, before I can stop myself.

"Does that fucking matter, Denise?" he snarls, this time pounding me so hard my stomach feels like it's colliding against the seat of the bench, even though they're already connected. He's smoking and spanking, somehow, as if he has all the time in the world, as if he isn't providing more than the tears I asked for, countless more.

"Yes. No. I don't know," I sob, wanting to rewind to the start of this scene. I try to let my mind go black, especially when he moves around to kiss me hard, his breath smoky. He pulls back and I sense him draw the cigarette right under my lips, close enough that I can feel the orange flame, before he moves it out away from me. This is a mean side of him I've never seen before, something beyond sadistic, like he wants to hurt me all the way through, not just make my ass quake and smolder.

"Well, it's none of your business. Not anymore," he says. He hasn't shackled me, yet I couldn't move even if I wanted to. The bench is my savior, my companion, my safety net. I keep thinking he's going to bust out some exquisite new toy, a wooden panel, a ruler, a cane. He likes to make me scream and flinch, to mark me, render me as his fully and completely. He likes that I'm into spanking, but always finds ways to make me feel like an amateur spankee who hasn't quite reached the levels of masochism his latest toy warrants. But this time, he goes back to that trusty favorite: his hand. He has ways of curving that body part that turn it into the sickest instrument around.

"Don't say a word, Denise. For once, just keep your fucking mouth shut." He sounds like someone else entirely; he's put on an accent to go with his words, Queens blue collar instead of his usual clipped, cultured, Westchester doctor voice. Yes, he loves playing doctor with me, another thing that'll have to end now, I suppose. "Good. I'm going to spank you until you're all cried out, and I'll be the judge of that."

Strangely, even though he starts with hardly any warm-up, just raises his hand like a whip and strikes me smartly across my cheeks, I can't cry just yet. I clamp my eyes shut, breathe through my nose, and focus on the pain. This I can process, this I can deal with, this I think I want. My pussy is getting wet and yet somehow I hardly feel it. "This not hard enough for you?" he asks, then digs his short but strong nails into my ass after one particularly rough blow.

This goes on for thirty-seven minutes. I know because he tells me; he's been looking at the clock, must want to get this over with already. I'm wondering why he doesn't just use a paddle or something already when I feel his hand hit me and then a burning sensation. He's added something to his palm that makes it sting like hell. Next he shoves what I'm sure is our metal dildo into my cunt. He plunges it in without any hesitation, then goes right on with the searing smacks that really feel like he's added chili pepper or something to his hand. It burns, and hurts, but I still open for him to fuck me with the toy, or rather, my pussy does. My head is still locked on what he's just revealed.

When an hour has passed and only one lone tear has dribbled down my cheek, he stands me up and then has me kneel before him. He takes off the blindfold. I want to look into his eyes, but I don't. I stare down at the ground, hardly knowing who he is anymore. Then he strikes me across the face. This isn't a loving tap or even a sexual smack. He hits me, just once, across my right cheek. He's a leftie, so it stings real good. "I got her a spanking machine. The one you always wanted. It's spanking her right now, warming up her ass just for me." He reaches for my nipple again, twisting it until I cry out. I wonder why he's telling me these things, why he's being so mean. I wonder if I'll have to move to avoid seeing the two of them around.

I picture her, then, her ass, a good one-third the size of mine, raised up on that sweet machine while it pummels her over and over and over again. Evan and I had gotten off watching women being spanked by those machines, and I'd been angling for one for months. Monique's new in town, was, I thought, a new friend. He's known her less than two months and already she's usurped my place. That's when the tears start, first a few on one side then a few on the other, weak little rivulets of saltwater. That's when Evan takes me across his lap, my favorite. He used to do it before bed sometimes, telling me he loved me while using the meanest wooden paddle we owned. Now he does it and I just let the tears fall onto the ground. At first I put my arm in my mouth to stifle my sobs, but then I just let loose. His smacks are no harder than before, but they feel harder, somehow. We both lose track of time as the spanking seems to go on forever, my cries only ending when he shoves four fat fingers into my pussy and smacks my ass some more. Finally, I'm all done. I've come in a quick, almost rebellious burst. I don't want to give him that satisfaction, but I can't resist his touch. I look up at him through the haze of tears, searching his eyes for an answer as my throbbing ass welcomes the cool air from the window.

When it's over, I try to sneak off to the bathroom, my face streaked with tears, my body seeming to sag under its own weight. I want to be alone, to curl up in the bath and merge into the bubbles. But he grabs me again, roughly, hugging me so tightly that at first I don't realize he has tears in his eyes, too, tears that are slowly sliding down his face. "What are you crying about?" I ask bitterly, selfishly liking the comfort of his solid strength.

"Dee, my sweet Dee. I'm not going anywhere. I'm yours. Forever, remember? But you wanted me to make you cry, and I knew I had to go far, far down to somewhere foreign and scary to really make you scared. You're a tough woman to crack, even though you don't always realize it."

I stare at him in disbelief, wondering whether he's an evil genius or a truly sick bastard. I guess part of why I love him is that I'll never truly have the answer to that, I just have to keep lowering myself to the depths of despair, and seeing if I make it through.

ABOUT THE AUTHORS

LAURA BACCHI is an author of erotica and erotic romance. Her work can be found at Ruthie's Club and in e-book format at Loose-Id, Samhain, Amber Quill Press, and Liquid Silver Books. Laura's erotic shorts will soon be in print in multiauthor anthologies from Pretty Things Press (*Screaming Orgasms and Sex on the Beach*) and Cleis (*Hard Hats*). For more about Laura, visit www.laurabacchi.com.

L. ELISE BLAND is a spanking and paddling aficionado. In fact, she owns as many paddles as she does pairs of shoes. Some of her publications include *Naughty Spanking Stories from A to Z 1* and *2*, *Best American Erotica 2006*, *First-Timers: True Stories of Lesbian Awakening* and *Best Lesbian Erotica 2008*. Learn more at www.lelisebland.com.

TENILLE BROWN's erotic fiction can be found in such anthologies as *Iridescence*, *Got a Minute*, *F Is for Fetish*, *Sex and Candy*, *J Is for*

Jealousy, and *Rubber Sex*. She is a staff writer for Custom Erotica Source and keeps various blogs on her website, www.tenillebrown. com and her MySpace page, www.myspace.com/tenillebrown.

THOMAS CHRISTOPHER has published stories in the *Louisville Review*, *Small Spiral Notebook*, the *MacGuffin*, *Cooweescoowee*, and *Redivider*. He holds an MFA from Western Michigan University and he was recently awarded an Irving S. Gilmore Emerging Artist Grant. You can read more of his work at www.thomaschristopher.com.

ELIZABETH COLDWELL is the editor of the UK edition of *Forum* magazine. Her work has appeared in a number of anthologies including *Best SM Erotica 1* and *2*, *Five Minute Fantasies 2* and *Spank Me*. She firmly believes that naughty boys need to learn their lesson.

SHANNA GERMAIN is a poet by nature, a short-story writer by the skin of her teeth, and a novelist in training. Her work has been published in places like *Absinthe Literary Review*, *Best American Erotica 2007*, *Best Gay Romance 2008*, *Best Lesbian Erotica 2008*, *Dirty Girls*, *He's on Top*, *Hide and Seek*, and *Tipton Poetry Review*. Visit her online at www.shannagermain.com.

MADELINE GLASS is a self-described "prim and properly perverted parent." Her sex blog, Madeline in the Mirror, was a finalist for Best Sex Blog by the Best of Blogs. She is a contributor at thesexcarnival.com, a past writer for porn site TGP.com, and a guest contributor to Fleshbot. Her book *Sex 365: A Position for Every Day* will be published in 2008. This is her first published piece of erotic fiction.

M. DAVID HORNBUCKLE is a full-time writer and musician, originally from Birmingham, Alabama. His fiction has been published in McSweeney's Internet Tendency, *Isms*, *Peek*, *Air in the Paragraph Line*, and *Astarte*. His novella *The Salvation of Billy Wayne Carter* was published as an e-book by Cantarabooks in October 2007. Hornbuckle now lives in New York City where he is finishing up a novel and is the leader of the M. David Hornbuckle Dixieland Space Orchestra.

ROSALIND CHRISTINE LLOYD lives with her queer version of a nuclear family in Soho, New York and up in the Catskill Mountains. Her work has appeared in more than fifteen erotic anthologies including *Best American Erotica* as well as *Best Lesbian Erotica*.

FIONA LOCKE is a very kinky girl. She has fantasized about spanking for as long as she can remember and she's been writing stories about it all her life. She feels there's simply nothing to compare with the warm glow of a smacked bottom. Her debut novel, *Over the Knee,* is a semiautobiographical account of her fantasies and experiences in the spanking scene. The publisher even convinced her to pose for the cover.

MADLYN MARCH is the pseudonym of a writer whose work has appeared in the anthology *First-Timers*, Black Table, After-Ellen, AfterElton, *Complete Woman*, the *New York Post, Time Out New York*, and others. Toni is based on a bully who once tortured her, but the sexual part is all wishful thinking.

ANDY OHIO is a writer in New York City. His writing has been published in various places including the anthologies *Slow Grind* and *Best Bisexual Erotica 2001*.

RICK ROBERTS works in book publishing and is an author of fiction and nonfiction. He lives in Connecticut.

TERESA NOELLE ROBERTS has turned speculating obsessively about sex into a career. Her erotica has appeared in *Caught Looking: Erotic Tales of Voyeurs and Exhibitionists, Ultimate Lesbian Erotica 2007, B Is for Bondage, E Is for Exotic, F Is for Fetish, H Is for Hardcore, He's on Top, She's on Top,* and other anthologies with equally provocative titles. She also writes with a coauthor under the name Sophie Mouette; look for Sophie's erotica in *Best Women's Erotica 2007,* Fishnetmag.com, *Caught Looking,* and various *Wicked Words* anthologies. Sophie's novel *Cat Scratch Fever* was published by Black Lace Books.

THOMAS S. ROCHE is the author of several hundred published erotic short stories as well as work in the horror, crime, fantasy, and science fiction genres. His published books include four anthologies of horror/fantasy, three books of erotic crime-noir, and three erotica collections. He is is the public relations manager of Kink.com, and blogs and podcasts on sex, drugs, and cryptozoology at Thomasroche.com as well as writing for Blowfish.com and Techyum.com.

SIMON SHEPPARD is the editor of *Homosex: Sixty Years of Gay Erotica* and the upcoming *Leathermen,* and the author of *In Deep: Erotic Stories; Kinkorama: Dispatches from the Front Lines of Perversion; Sex Parties 101;* and *Hotter Than Hell and Other Stories.* His work also appears in more than two hundred and fifty anthologies, including many editions of *Best American Erotica* and *Best Gay Erotica.* He writes the syndicated column "Sex Talk" and the online serial "The Dirty Boys Club," and hangs out at www.simonsheppard.com.

DONNA GEORGE STOREY's erotic fiction has appeared in *She's on Top, He's on Top, Sexiest Soles, Sex and Candy, Garden of the Perverse, E Is for Exotic, Taboo, Best American Erotica 2006, Mammoth Book of Best New Erotica 4, 5, 6* and *7,* and *Best Women's Erotica 2005, 2006, 2007,* and *2008.* Her novel set in Japan, *Amorous Woman,* is part of Orion's Neon erotica series. Read more of her work at www.DonnaGeorgeStorey.com.

Called "a trollop with a laptop" by *East Bay Express,* and a "literary siren" by Good Vibrations, **ALISON TYLER** is naughty and she knows it. Ms. Tyler is the author of more than twenty-five explicit novels, and the editor of thirty-six anthologies including *A Is for Amour, B Is for Bondage, C Is for Coeds, D Is for Dress-Up, E Is for Exotic, F Is for Fetish, G Is for Games,* and *H Is for Hardcore.* In all things important, Ms. Tyler remains faithful to her partner of more than a decade, but she still can't choose just one perfume. Visit her at www.alisontyler.com or be her friend at www.myspace.com/alisontyler.

SAGE VIVANT is the author of *Your Erotic Personality* and founder of Custom Erotica Source (www.customeroticasource. com). She has edited several anthologies with partner M. Christian: *The Best of Both Worlds, Confessions, Amazons,* and *Garden of the Perverse.* In addition to hosting the podcast, "Four Minutes, Once a Week" since September 2005, she is also the author of the novel *Giving the Bride Away.* Her stories have been published in dozens of anthologies.

ABOUT
THE EDITOR

RACHEL KRAMER BUSSEL (www.rachelkramerbussel.com) is an author, editor, blogger, and reading series host. She has edited or coedited more than twenty books of erotica, including *Naughty Spanking Stories 1* and *2; Yes, Sir; Yes, Ma'am; He's on Top; She's on Top; Caught Looking; Hide and Seek; Crossdressing; Rubber Sex; Sex and Candy; Ultimate Undies; Glamour Girls; Bedding Down;* and the nonfiction collection *Best Sex Writing 2008.* Her work has been published in more than one hundred anthologies, including *Best American Erotica 2004* and *2006,* Zane's *Succulent: Chocolate Flava II* and *Purple Panties, Everything You Know About Sex Is Wrong, Single State of the Union,* and *Desire: Women Write About Wanting.* Her first novel, *Everything But...,* will be published by Bantam. She serves as senior editor at *Penthouse Variations,* and wrote the popular "Lusty Lady" column for the *Village Voice.*

Rachel has written for *AVN, Bust, Curve,* Fresh Yarn, Gothamist, Huffington Post, Mediabistro, *Newsday, New York*

Post, Penthouse, Playgirl, San Francisco Chronicle, Time Out New York, and *Zink,* among others. She has been quoted in the *New York Times, USA Today, Maxim UK, Glamour UK, GQ Italy, National Post (Canada), Wysokie Obcasy* (Poland), *Seattle Weekly,* and other publications, and has appeared on the *Martha Stewart Show, Berman and Berman Show,* NY1, and Showtime's *Family Business.* She has hosted In the Flesh Erotic Reading Series since October 2005, about which the *New York Times's* "UrbanEye" newsletter said she "welcomes eroticism of all stripes, spots, and textures." She blogs at lustylady.blogspot.com and cupcakestakethecake.blogspot.com.